MURDER GOES CAROLING

A PIPER HAYDN PIANO MYSTERY

MALISSA CHAPIN

IVORY KEYS PRESS

*For my precious friends Alissa, Anissa, Crystal, and Michele
Thanking God for your friendship and support, but wishing
we had met on a different path.*

***S**till, still, still,*
One can hear the falling snow.
For all is hushed,
The world is sleeping,
Holy Star its vigil keeping.
Still, still, still,
One can hear the falling snow.
Sleep, sleep, sleep,
'Tis the eve of our Saviour's birth.
The night is peaceful all around you,
Close your eyes,
Let sleep surround you.
Sleep, sleep, sleep,
'Tis the eve of our Saviour's birth.

Austrian Christmas Carol 1865

Prologue

None of this would have happened if I hadn't organized the Caroling Extravaganza.

CHAPTER 1

Still, still still, one can hear the falling snow.

Thursday

A swirl of stinging snowflakes whipped around Piper Haydn as she battled Wisconsin's winter. Her eyes and nose tingled from the below zero temps, and she tightened the scarf around her neck as she shivered.

Good thing mom knows how to knit a cozy scarf. Winter had taken over Wisconsin far too early this year, and Piper feared the frigid temperatures might sabotage the Cranberry Harbor Christkindlmarket. The outdoor Christmas market opened in two weeks, and Piper had a mile-long list of details to work out before opening day. And she still had to oversee the tree lighting ceremony and the Caroling Extravaganza this weekend.

She'd corral the teachers at her music academy and her best friend, Roosevelt Hale, to help accomplish the endless tasks. But first something to warm her insides. A bell jingled overhead as Piper ducked into the Tea Thyme shop. The pungent aroma of tea and herbs tickled her icy nose.

"Piper," Maisy called from behind the counter. "Good afternoon. What brings you out today? It's positively brutal out there."

"Maisy, I require something hot to thaw me or I shan't continue venturing down the way."

"It's so cold you turned into a Puritan?" Maisy laughed. "But I agree. I've shivered all day and keep gulping tea. I keep my icy fingers cuddling this." She held a thick pottery mug to her lips and sipped.

Piper peeled her gloves off one finger at a time, dropping them on the counter. "Where did this deep freeze come from? I wasn't paying attention to the weather report. Did you know the weather was supposed to drop below zero so soon?"

"No. I didn't pay attention either, but at least it's not as bitter cold as the last polar vortex Wisconsin sent us."

Piper groaned. "Don't dredge up awful memories. At least we can function in these temperatures. Remember when they canceled mail delivery last time?"

"I know." Maisy shivered. "I'm worried no one will come out if it doesn't warm up soon. I'm sure the temperature will ease up long before the Christkindlmarket though. How's your to-do list coming along?"

A cross between a groan and a squeak rushed from Piper. "Please don't remind me. I'm up to my eyeballs in details and I'm don't think the chores will ever end."

"You'll get everything done, and we'll celebrate like the fine, fun-loving folks we are." Maisy arranged a cinnamon apple butter scone on a dainty gold rimmed saucer, and slid the treat across the counter. She filled a teacup decorated with holly and berries with steaming tea. "Eat. You need hot tea and carbs to fortify you while you navigate the frozen tundra."

Piper rested in an overstuffed chair in the corner. "You have no idea. You're the best, Maisy. What is Tea Thyme selling at the Christkindlmarket?"

Maisy's eyes sparkled. "Right now, I'm busy testing holiday blends—spicy concoctions with cinnamon and berries—and packaging the tea in gold tins. Rosie is painting the product labels for me, and hand lettering 'Cranberry Harbor Christkindlmarket' across the top."

"Ooh. I look forward to sampling your amazing recipes." Piper drained her tea, gulped the last piece of scone, and grinned. "I know. Not very ladylike. Please don't tell my mother."

Maisy grinned. "My lips are sealed, friend."

Piper tugged on her gloves and bundled up, twisting the scarf tightly around her face. "I'll catch up later. Oh, did the Earl Grey tea I ordered for my dad's gift arrive?"

"I expect the shipment on Friday. I'll call you."

"Thanks."

"Stay warm," Maisy called.

"Bye," Piper called as she stepped out of the cozy tea shop. The brisk wind whistled down Main Street, blowing against Piper and stinging her eyes. She rushed down the sidewalk to Cassidy's yarn store, wondering why she hadn't stayed home bundled in her quilt this morning. A crackling fire, a steaming mug of tea, and a well-written novel beckoned her home. Anything seemed better than battling this arctic cold. But she had Christmas gifts to purchase and vendor details to confirm. *Why I offered to lead the market this year, I'll never know. Sign up to lead the market, they said. It will be fun, they said.*

She rushed through the entry of the Wooly Llama, and the door slammed behind her. "Hello, Cassidy," Piper called as she wiped her snow boots on the doormat.

"What are you doing out, Piper? The weather is ridiculous."

"Business."

"I'm doing business too, but don't tell anyone my secret." She leaned across the counter and whispered, "I cozy up with an afghan while I knit." Cassidy smiled. "Let's sit in my classroom. You look like you need to thaw."

Piper joined Cassidy on the sofa and accepted the plush afghan her friend held out. She wrapped the blanket around her shoulders and melted into the couch. "Today is my only day off this week, and I am checking in with the market vendors and choosing gifts for my family. Speaking of gifts...do you suggest I purchase yarn for my mother's knitting obsession or a gift certificate and let her choose her present?"

Cassidy tapped her chin and frowned. "What about a bag full of fun knitting tools and organizers?"

"Perfect," Piper said. "Can you put a gift together and call me with the total? Oh, by the way, what are you selling at the market?"

"Red and green yarn bundles and an easy yarn star ornament kit for those who don't knit or crochet."

"Perfect," Piper said. She leaned her head against the plush couch and closed her eyes. "Think I'll stay put and take a nap. Battling the wind zaps my energy."

Cassidy laughed. "You're not the first person to nap in my classroom. Stay all day if you like."

Piper sat up and folded the heavy afghan. "If I don't keep moving, I'll never finish these errands. Don is pulling the nativity set out of storage today, so I'm on my way to open the academy for him."

Cassidy clapped her hands. "I love the nativity scene. The carving and painting on the figures are exquisite. For once, Mr. Standerwick did something nice by donating the set to Cranberry Harbor."

"For some odd reason, Rosie likes the old curmudgeon. She says he's not so bad."

"Rosie doesn't think anyone is bad. How is her job going?"

"She enjoys working for Fergus, but she only works a couple of days a week doing miscellaneous chores."

"Well, good for her. Perhaps she can soften the old man up a little. Speaking of men..."

Piper held her hand up. "I know where you're going. And no. Nothing's happening."

Cassidy frowned. "I thought you and Chief Maxwell were an item."

"One date, Cassidy. Dinner. Nothing else."

Her friend stared and put her hands on her hips. "Piper Haydn. Tell me you did not chase Will away?"

Piper frowned.

"Piper?" Her friend raised an eyebrow.

"I'm busy, Cassidy. I'm not a teenager all googly-eyed over a boy. No time for dating."

Cassidy pursed her lips. "Girl."

"Don't 'girl' me. I don't need your icy stare freezing my insides too. My outsides are cold enough as it is."

Cassidy laughed, rubbing her fingers across Piper's knit scarf. "Ooh, your mom used the luscious merino wool on this one. The cherry red compliments your coat perfectly."

"Keeps me warm. Well, relatively speaking. Nothing keeps me warm on a day like today."

"Don't stay out too long. I don't want to read about you on The Cranberry Harbor Tattler tonight."

"Oh, boy. Where did the blog come from?"

"No one knows." Cassidy raised her eyebrows. "It's all a big mystery," she said, mimicking the voice of a narrator in a terrifying movie.

"I hope we find out who's behind it." She tucked the ends of the wool scarf into her coat. "I promise I'll head home after one more stop. The rest of the day, I'm plunking down in my turret to drink steaming hot beverages and read 'til bedtime."

"Good girl. Catch you later."

Cranberry Harbor residents hunker down as an arctic blast sweeps through Wisconsin. Chief Maxwell requests that all citizens stay home. According to weather forecasters, the dangerously cold temperatures should move out in the next day or two. Just in time for the Caroling Extravaganza that some residents enjoy. The rest of us wish you'd leave us alone. The Cranberry Harbor Tattler

"Hello," Becky called when Piper blew through the front door of The Kindred Spirits Bookshop. "What in the world are you doing out in this weather?"

Piper unwound her wool scarf and wiped tears from her eyes. "My goodness! The wind makes my eyes water."

"Don't I know it? The cold air whistles right through my display window. The weather report said one more day of this, then we should see warmer temperatures. I hope they arrive before the Caroling Extravaganza on Saturday."

Piper laughed. "Do you mean warmer temps for the rest of the states or warmer for Wisconsin?"

"Exactly, brr." Becky laughed and rubbed her arms. "How can I help you?"

"I'm shopping for Christmas gifts for my three little nephews and checking in with all the Christkindlmarket vendors."

Becky's eyes sparkled. "Oh, I love the market. Thank you for taking over the planning. I thought we'd need to skip this year when no one stepped up to take charge."

"I'm praying for another volunteer to take over next year. I cannot handle all these details." She grimaced. "We should appoint a committee rather than dumping this much work on one person."

"Good idea. Add it to your list," Becky said. "For the market, I'm selling an assortment of children's Christmas books, a few classics for adults, along with bookmarks and fun literary accessories."

"Perfect. What about my nephews? Asher is all about soccer. Landon still loves teddy bears and big trucks, and baby Zeke chews everything."

Becky laughed. "Good thing I sell board books. Do you want me to gather fun books for the boys or would you like to choose the titles?

Piper checked the clock above the counter. "I'm opening the academy for Don. He's digging the nativity scene out of storage today. After that, I'm curling up in my turret with a book and blanket. Can you choose the books and call me when they're ready for pickup?"

"Absolutely. And hey, thanks again for organizing the market. Christmas season wouldn't be the same without it. The Caroling Extravaganza is my absolute favorite, though. I'm so glad we take time to visit the shut-ins and spread Christmas joy."

"You're a sweetheart, Becky." Piper wound her scarf around her neck and buttoned her coat.

"I may be a sweetheart, but my singing voice is sour. I pity everyone forced to listen to me." She grinned. "But I never stop singing."

Piper laughed. "The Bible instructs us to 'make a joyful noise'. I'm fairly certain most of Cranberry Harbor makes joyful noises when they carol. But you're right, sharing Christmas joy makes every minute spent organizing the market and the Caroling Extravaganza worth my time."

"Will you see Rosie today? She's painting labels for my stickers and I have new ideas. Can you have her call me?"

"Sure thing. Stay warm." Piper stepped out into the cold, amazed at herself for leaving her house this morning. Anticipating the heated seats in her Mercedes, she shivered and rushed down the street.

Piper parked at the Haydn Music Academy as Don stepped out of his pickup truck and joined her inside the front door. She blew on her numb fingers and rubbed her hands together.

"I apologize for calling you out on this frigid day, Don. We should have pulled the nativity set out of storage before the freezing weather blew in."

"Not a problem, Piper. We have two weeks to prepare for the Christkindlmarket, but if I don't start on the nativity scene today, I'll never get it done. I want to clean the figures and examine the pieces for defects before we move them to the park."

"I appreciate your hard work. Can you lock up? I'd like to head home and snuggle in." She twisted a key off her keyring and handed it to him.

"I'll call when I'm leaving. When should I deliver the figures to the park?"

"Next week. The parks department is building a new crèche after last year's market fiasco."

Don chuckled. "Kids. I don't think they meant any harm, but at least the figures are safe."

"For sure. If anything happens to the nativity set while Fergus is alive, his wrath will force everyone to move out of Cranberry Harbor."

"True, but donating the set to Cranberry Harbor for all to enjoy was incredibly thoughtful of him."

"All I know about Fergus is how much he despises my family," Piper said, remembering the curmudgeon's tirades and all the times he shook his shovel at her and her brothers. "Do you know him well?"

"Nah. No one knows Fergus very well. What does Rosie say? Doesn't she work for him?"

"News travels fast around here, huh?" Piper raised an eyebrow. "Yeah. She does odd jobs at his house twice a week. She says Fergus is a big teddy bear under his curmudgeonly shell."

"Well, Rosie seems to be an excellent judge of character. You should trust her." He stepped toward the front door. "I need to finish up. My wife started dinner in the crock pot and I never miss a chance to eat her roast beef."

Piper laughed. "Hurry home then, but call me if you need anything."

"I'll leave the figures in the back hallway to keep them safe until I deliver them. Be careful out there."

"You too, Don," Piper called, scurrying to her car.

Piper pulled her scarf over her nose when she stepped out of the car. She ran to her back door, but stopped to spread salt across the sidewalk. Salt wouldn't melt ice at these cold temperatures, but the grit might offer traction. She breathed a sigh of relief when she stepped inside her home, closing the door against the frozen air. She couldn't wait to curl up on her couch with an afghan—divine. Turning on the flame under her tea kettle, she waited near the stove, planning her cozy evening at home. A crackling fire in the turret fireplace, a book, and an evening resting on her couch seemed ideal. The book she'd started the other day had reached a cliffhanger, and she couldn't wait to find out how the author would rescue the heroine.

Piper burrowed under the blanket with her cup of tea and her book, settling in for a long winter nap. A few moments later, banging on the front door interrupted her reading, and she threw the blanket off her still chilly body and slipped into her plush slippers before her toes touched the icy floor.

"I'm coming," she hollered when the banging increased. Rosie peered in the window, face pressed against the glass, rolling her eyes and licking the window.

"For crying out loud, Roosevelt. You're leaving marks on my window and you're going to freeze your tongue to the glass."

Rosie laughed and stepped into Piper's entryway, peeling off bulky layers of winter gear. "My goodness. It's fridgediculous out there."

"New word?"

"Made it up this very morning. Perfect word for this weather, right? Brr." She shivered and hung her coat on the hook near Piper's front door. She straightened the seams of a white ruffled blouse and tugged a red cable-knit sweater vest over her yellow leggings. Red and green jingle bell earrings glittered in her ears. Rosie rubbed her hands together. "Tea kettle hot?"

"Yes, but I'm going back to snuggle under my blanket. Help yourself." Piper covered her legs with the blanket and sipped tea. "Where'd you get the outfit? Yellow leggings and Christmas colors?"

"Come on, it looks great. I thrifted this at Cranberry Closet, as always. Fabulous, huh?" Rosie's earrings jingled down the hall as she skipped to the kitchen. Cupboard doors slammed, and she hollered at the top of her lungs, "You want something to eat? Looks like you have yummy snacks in here."

Piper laughed. "Sure. You twisted my arm. Grab those muffins from Dominque."

Rosie walked into the turret, a mug in one hand, a bag of chips under her arm, and a box of muffins from Sweetberry's. She lifted the lid and sniffed. "What flavor did Dominique bake today?" She handed Piper the box. "Scooch. I need a spot." She sank into the cushions on the end of the couch and snatched the corner of Piper's blanket, tugging the cozy warmth around her shoulders.

"Hey, give me back my blanket. Get your own from the basket." Piper shrieked when Rosie rested icy feet on her leg.

Rosie laughed. "See. I told you it's fridgediculous. Please don't make me find another blanket. You already warmed this one up. Come on, let me share."

"Fine, but keep your icy toes away from me."

"Deal," Rosie said. "Any news?" She munched on a muffin and licked her fingers.

"Don is retrieving the nativity figures from storage today. Becky wants you to call her. Something about labels you're painting. How are you managing commissions, working at the academy and working for Fergus, too?"

"Pfft. Working for Fergus is easy. I move his stuff around and dust things." She reached into the box for another muffin. "His sister-in-law is coming for Christmas, so I'll have time off 'til she leaves."

"Sister-in-law? I didn't know he had any relatives other than his sons."

"Mrs. Standerwick's long-lost sister—or something. I have no idea. Fergus doesn't talk to me. He grunts and disappears when I'm around."

"Discover any interesting stuff over there?"

"Well, the other day, I *accidentally* dusted inside the dresser drawers in his guest room and found an old diary and some ancient papers. Most were German or some language, but a few were English. Want to know what I read?"

"Rosie!"

"What?"

"Accidentally dusted inside his drawers?" Piper gasped. "You can't read private letters and journals. What if he finds out?"

"Never fear. I put everything back in the drawer exactly how I found it."

"No! Don't tell me anything. I'm not taking part in your snooping."

Rosie laughed, burrowing under the blanket. She finished the cinnamon streusel muffin and nudged Piper's leg with her toes. "What are you reading?"

Piper peeked over the top of the book. "Not sure. I'm having difficulty concentrating right now." She cleared her throat. "But if you must know, I was reading a thriller when I was home alone, but after *someone* interrupted me, I grabbed this memoir of Handel written by his friend."

"Fancy," Rosie said. "Anything interesting?"

Piper closed one eye and stared at Rosie. "Sure. Right here, the author says that Handel and another gentleman had a disagreement. When the other gentleman stabbed George, the musical score inside his coat saved him from injury."

"Amazing," Rosie said. Pretending to zip her lips, she picked up a home décor magazine from the side table and flipped through several pages. "Your remodel turned out nice. You happy?"

"Yes," Piper said, concentrating on her reading.

"What's our next project?"

Piper sighed and closed the book. "I haven't decided. My brain's frozen right now. After the Christkindlmarket, I'll choose a project soon, but I'm not planning to start any extensive work before spring. We need ventilation if we paint or tear down walls. I considered calling a contractor for an estimate on the main staircase and those squeaky steps."

"No way. The squeak is your security system. If someone sneaks up your stairs during the night, they'll step on the squeaky stairs. Tada! Then you call Chief Maxwell to the rescue."

"I won't call Chief Maxwell for anything."

"Oh, come on, Piper. He definitely likes you. Give him a chance."

"I did. We went out for dinner."

Rosie rolled her eyes and hopped up. "I'm refilling my tea. Want anything?"

Piper lifted the blanket and pulled the fluffy fabric up to her chin. "Hot cocoa, please. The mix is in the cupboard above the coffee pot."

Rosie grimaced. "I don't understand how you can eat chocolate *and* drink the stuff. Gross."

"Oh, Rosie, you're missing out on one of the great joys in life."

Rosie marched to the kitchen, and Piper opened her book. She'd read half of a chapter when her phone rang.

"Piper!" Don's voice roared. "Come quick. There's been a murder."

Piper dropped her book and stammered. "What? What did you say?"

Rosie stood in the doorway, her eyes wide.

"A murder."

"Hang up. Call 9-1-1!" Visions of her ex-fiancé inside her newly delivered Steinway piano and the body in the campfire ring in Door County flashed through her mind. Her stomach twisted, and blood drained from her face.

"I'm...I'm sorry, Piper. Let me rephrase. Not a body, but hurry. I'm in the storage area." The phone clicked off, and Piper tossed the blanket aside, jumping from the couch.

"Hurry. Get your coat, Rosie. I'll drive. Call the police on the way."

Piper backed out of the driveway, her heart pounding.

"What do you think he meant?" Rosie said, jerking the seat belt across her chest.

"He said murder. What else can he mean? Call Chief Maxwell. Tell him we're on the way to the academy."

Rosie punched in the number and Piper scanned the side streets as she breezed through stop signs. She prayed she'd notice any icy patches before the tires hit slick spots. She didn't want to slide into a ditch. Her heart pounded, and she gripped the steering wheel to keep her hands from shaking. She careened onto the sidewalk in front of Haydn Music Academy and they jumped out, slamming car doors as they ran to the entrance.

Piper's breath blew out in wispy clouds around her face and tiny ice crystals formed in her nose. She'd left the house so quickly, she hadn't grabbed her scarf. She shoved a key into the lock and yanked on the handle with stiff fingers. Rosie ran behind Piper, her breath blowing out in loud huffs as they ran toward the storage room.

"What did the police say?" Piper flipped on lights.

"They're on the way and we're supposed to stay outside," Rosie said.

"Too late." Piper ran ahead of Rosie, shouting, "Don! Don!" A muffled voice and banging rang out, and Rosie clutched Piper's arm.

"Maybe we *should* wait for Chief Maxwell."

Piper stopped and held her chest as she gasped for breath. Several more clunks, and a loud shriek echoed through the hall.

Rosie's eyes widened, and she froze. "Piper, maybe we should wait here."

Voices rang out behind them. "Miss Haydn? Miss Hale? Police."

"Down here. In the hall," Rosie shouted.

Footsteps pounded, and Chief Maxwell and several officers rounded the corner. He ran past the women. "Where to?"

Piper pointed. "Storage room."

"Stay there until I call for you," Chief Maxwell yelled as he ran. The officers ran past, and Piper narrowed her eyes.

"I'm not standing around waiting for a call in my own academy." She grasped Rosie's hand, and they ran behind the officers, Rosie's earrings jingling all the way.

Don stood in the center of the storage room, his hands in the air. Officers swarmed the room yelling, "Don't move!"

Piper and Rosie halted in the doorway, squeezing each other's hands. Piper's heart pounded in her ears and she gasped, trying to slow her breathing.

"Do you see a body?" Rosie whispered.

Piper shook her head. "No, but Don is dripping blood."

Rosie gasped. "What are they saying?"

"Shh. They'll kick us out."

"Clear," Chief Maxwell shouted, and Don dropped his hands. "What's going on here?"

Don stared at the officers, his eyes wide. "I'm not sure. You tell me."

"Someone called in a murder at the Haydn Academy. Was it you?"

Don gulped. "No. I called Piper and said there's been a murder, but I didn't call 9-1-1."

"Where's the body?"

Don pointed to a heap of debris on the floor. "In hindsight, I should have chosen a different word."

Piper tip-toed into the storage area, Rosie close behind. "Don. You scared me half to death. You're bleeding."

Chief Maxwell spun around. "I told you two to stay back." He glared at Piper.

She stared, raising her chin. "This is *my* academy, Chief Maxwell. I need to know what's happening."

"You need to learn how to obey orders."

Rosie whistled behind Piper. "Yikes, he's brave," she whispered.

Piper glared at Chief Maxwell but held her tongue. "Can we sort this out?" She pointed at Don and handed him a roll of paper toweling from a shelf of cleaning supplies.

Chief Maxwell cleared his throat. "Don?"

"The parks department needed me to pull the nativity from storage this week, but I didn't have time before today." He pressed the paper towel to his hand. "When I opened the door, I found the nativity set in pieces all over the floor." He bent and snatched the decapitated head of a Wise Man, holding it out in his hands. "This one sliced my hand when I grabbed it," he said, pointing to the jagged edges on the piece.

Rosie giggled. "John the Baptist, anyone?"

"Shhh." Piper warned. She stepped further into the room and gasped. "Oh, no." She dropped to her knees near the pile. Wise Men lay on their sides, animals lay face down. Limbs, heads, and crowns lay scattered around the room.

"Don't touch," Chief Maxwell ordered.

Piper jumped and twisted her hands. "I didn't think."

"Everyone step back." He pointed to the doorway. "Over there, you two."

Piper and Rosie moved to the doorway as the chief fired questions at Don.

"Was the door locked?"

"I don't remember."

"Were the lights on?"

"No."

"Was anything else disturbed?"

"Not that I noticed."

"Who has access to this area?"

Don thought for a moment. "Piper and I. Who else?"

"Miss Haydn?"

Piper closed her eyes, thinking of her staff. "The keys hang in our reception office. I don't remember sending other staff down here. Don's the only one I know of. Anyone can use the keys, though. It's not a restricted area—only junk storage."

Chief Maxwell pointed at the pile of debris. "What is this, and why is it here?"

"Fergus Standerwick donated this nativity to Cranberry Harbor, but after we displayed it in the park last Christmas, the city needed a place to store the figures. We have this huge storage area, so I offered the space." She glanced around the room. "I can't imagine why anyone would break in and damage this."

Don scratched his head. "Did the thieves knock over the nativity set while searching for something else?"

"What do you store in here, Miss Haydn?" a deputy interrupted. He pulled out a notebook and pen.

"Play props, old sheet music, extra furniture, chalkboards, books, miscellaneous things leftover from the old school. I can't think of anything valuable."

"What about the nativity set?" Chief Maxwell pointed at the rubble.

Piper frowned. "It's an old dusty set. Nothing special."

The deputy stepped closer to the broken figures. "How many pieces are in the set?"

"I'm not sure. Do you remember, Rosie?"

Rosie tapped her finger on her lips and narrowed her eyes. "Let's see. Are you writing this down?"

The deputy nodded.

"Mary, Joseph, Baby Jesus, three Wise Men." She faced Chief Maxwell and frowned. "Why do all the nativity scenes have three Wise Men? How could three dudes greatly trouble evil old King Herod?"

Piper nudged Rosie. "Not the time to discuss Bible history."

"Right," Rosie said. "Two donkeys, a camel, three sheep, three shepherds, and a treasure chest with the gold, frankincense, and myrrh."

The deputy counted. "Sixteen pieces, sir."

Chief Maxwell pointed to the pile of figures. "Thirteen? Everyone else count thirteen?"

The officers stepped up and counted. "Thirteen, Chief."

"They stole Mary, Baby Jesus, and the treasure chest," Rosie said, her hands on her hips and a scowl on her face. "What kind of creep steals Baby Jesus?"

Piper stepped closer to Chief Maxwell. "I don't think this is a police matter. We'll clean everything up and your officers can get back to their duties."

"Not so fast." He held up a hand. "An intruder broke into your storage area and destroyed town property, absconding with three figures. We'll investigate before we dismiss this incident as nothing." He sent the officers to search the storage area for clues or disturbances. He bent over the pile of figures and slipped gloves on.

While Piper, Rosie, and Don waited, the chief stood the figures on their bases lining up broken pieces in front of each one.

"I can understand why you used the word 'murder', Don. Kinda looks like one to me," Rosie whispered.

Don grimaced. "I accept responsibility for my poor choice of words, but when I opened the door and found a pile of heads and bodies, my brain short-circuited. Somebody did a number on the nativity."

Piper rested a hand on his arm. "When my heart rate settles down, I'll forgive you."

Rosie's eyes sparkled. "I prefer this type of murder scene to the real thing."

Piper shivered and closed her eyes as the image of Daniel's body in her Steinway flashed before her eyes. "Don't remind me. Seriously."

Rosie hugged Piper. "Cheer up, friend. We can deal with this. Small potatoes."

Piper smiled, but a chill unrelated to the weather lodged in her heart. *Would Daniel's betrayal always sting?*

After an hour of searching, Chief Maxwell and the officers cleared the rooms. No other disturbances.

"If you see anything or think of something, call me, Miss Haydn."

Piper nodded.

"Um," Rosie said.

Chief Maxwell turned. "Yes, Miss Hale?"

"Who's telling Fergus?"

"Telling Fergus what?" he frowned.

Rosie gestured with her hand around the room. "This."

Piper's eyes widened. "Not me."

"I nominate you, Don. You're the one who found his nativity set in this condition."

Don held up his hands. "No way. My wife has dinner waiting, and I'm not in the mood to deal with Fergus today."

"Dealing with Fergus?" Chief Maxwell rubbed his chin. "Good grief, what's the problem?"

"Fergus donated the nativity to Cranberry Harbor," Piper said. "but we don't understand why. He despises everyone in this town, but he did. And now..."

"Now he's gonna flip," Rosie said.

"Then I'll tell him." The chief ran his hands through his hair. "You know where he lives?"

The officer nodded. "Of course. Everyone knows where Fergus lives, but I'm not going with you, right?"

"You can run into a crime scene and confront criminals, but you can't inform an elderly man about damage to a nativity set?"

"Exactly," he said.

Piper, Rosie, and Don nodded.

Chief Maxwell looked between them and huffed. "This is ridiculous."

"It's fridgediculous too," Rosie said, clamping her hands over her mouth as the chief turned and glared at her. "What? It *is.*"

"How about you ride along with me, Miss Hale? You seem to find this situation amusing."

"Are you making me?" she squeaked.

He closed the notepad and stuffed it in his coat pocket. "I'd appreciate your cooperation, please."

Rosie pouted and looked at Piper. "Help," she whispered.

Piper stepped back. "No way. You're on your own. You know Fergus anyway."

"Miss Hale?"

"I do odd jobs for him a few days a week. We're not friends or anything. He disappears when I'm working."

"How do you get paid?"

"He leaves money on the counter," Rosie said.

"I don't think anyone knows Fergus," Don said. "Not really. He's an enigma. Hiding in his mansion and only coming outside to yell at poor kids passing by."

"Or shake his shovel at them," Piper said.

"You'd like me to believe Cranberry Harbor is afraid of a hermit?"

"Not afraid, exactly," Don said.

Piper nodded. "Yes, not afraid. We just choose to avoid him."

"Alright, I get the picture. Miss Hale, will you consider accompanying me to inform him?"

"Of course, Chief Maxell, I'm delighted to accompany you." She clasped her hands and fluttered her eyelashes. "May I have a junior deputy badge? Pretty please."

"Rosie!" Piper admonished. She widened her eyes, signaling a warning to her friend. She watched Chief Maxwell, afraid of his reaction to her friend's impertinence.

"No. No junior deputy badge. Can we get going? I'll drop you off at home when we're done. Are you leaving, Miss Haydn?" he asked.

"Yes. I apologize for reporting a murder."

"No apology necessary. Doing my job. Let's go, Miss Hale."

"Yes, sir," Rosie called. "I'll have him drop me off at your place and fill you in."

"Your car is at my house anyway, Rosie."

"Good point." She squeezed Piper and buttoned her coat.

"Miss Hale," Chief Maxwell called from the hallway.

"Yikes," Rosie said, dashing into the hallway to catch up.

The frigid temperatures didn't explain the frosty atmosphere in the cruiser. Rosie sat in the front seat biting her lip, waiting for Chief Maxwell to say something—anything. When they'd driven several blocks in silence, Rosie blurted, "Why haven't you invited Piper on another date?"

Chief Maxwell tapped the steering wheel and drove a few blocks, his jaw clenched.

Rosie squirmed in her seat, berating herself for her big mouth. *Piper's gonna disown me this time.*

"I don't believe she's interested, Rosie."

Rosie laughed. "So you *can* call me Rosie."

"You can call me Will too, you know. I thought we were friends."

"Can't call you Will when you're doing police business. Weird."

He smiled. "Precisely why I called you Miss Hale. But back to your question. Miss Haydn isn't interested, and I'm not sitting around waiting for her to decide what she wants. I'm too old."

Rosie snorted. "You're not old. Come on. How old are you?"

"You haven't noticed my gray hair?"

"Nah. My mom had gray hair when I was a kid. Of course, she blames my brothers."

"Definitely not you?" He grinned.

"Definitely not me. You didn't answer, by the way."

"Thirty-seven."

"You're not much older than Piper. Well, a smidge. But who cares? Age doesn't matter once you're adults."

"You have life figured out, huh?"

"Not my life, but everyone else's. I have opinions."

Will laughed. "You're a treasure, Rosie. Never let anyone tell you otherwise."

"Thank you very much, kind sir. Now, about Piper."

Chief Maxwell hummed a Christmas jingle, increasing the volume when Rosie stared at him.

"You're not answering?"

He hummed louder, but a grin spread across his face.

"Fine. She'll have my hide for saying this, but I think you should ask her out again."

"Thanks for the advice."

"You're not gonna listen, are you?"

He hummed the jingle again, and Rosie let the conversation lull.

When they turned onto Fergus' street, Rosie pointed. "The big one. This driveway here."

He turned the cruiser into the driveway and parked in front of the house. Rosie hopped out, joining him on the porch as he rang the doorbell.

Piper leaned across the keyboard and scribbled on her score of Handel's *Messiah*. She shuffled sheet music and wrote notes in the margins. What possessed her to agree to lead the annual Caroling Extravaganza, the tree lighting ceremony *and* the Christkindlmarket? She already had piles of music to perform and lead at the academy. She led the church choir for the Christmas season, the community choir, the carolers, and the academy's children's choir. Church responsibilities and her personal to-do list piled on top of her commitment to oversee the Christkindlmarket.

She stared out the window and shuddered. *What's taking Chief Maxwell so long?* Fergus would sue her. She knew it. The ancient curmudgeon wouldn't miss an opportunity to punish a Haydn. His feud with her family went back decades before she was born.

She ran her finger across the keys, practicing several measures before she dropped her hands on the piano in frustration. She stood from the bench, closed the lid over the black and white keys, and paced back and forth in her turret. "Come on, Rosie. I need to know what I'm facing here."

Her phone rang.

"Piper," her mother's voice floated through the phone, "what's going on? Braden called and said Emily read on The Cranberry Harbor Tattler about the police swarming your academy this afternoon. What happened?"

"The Tattler? Who's writing this trash?" Piper gritted her teeth. "Why can't the small-minded gossips in this town find a better hobby?"

"Who cares *who* is writing it? I want to know what's going on."

Piper's phone beeped, and she peeked at the screen. "Dad's calling, Mom."

"Fill me in and I'll call him back."

Piper relayed the day's unfortunate events.

Her mother groaned. "I don't like this. I don't like any of this. Who would do something so terrible at Christmas time?"

"I have no idea, but I'm concerned about Fergus' reaction."

"Let your father and Braden handle Fergus."

"But we store the nativity at my building," she groaned. "He's going to lose his mind."

"Take a deep breath. Nothing is as bad as it seems at first. Right?"

Piper wanted to believe her mother. But...Fergus. "I'll try, Mom. You need to call Dad. He's calling again."

She pressed the button on her phone and opened her laptop to search for the new Cranberry Harbor blog. "Who writes this thing?" She searched the header and footer, but found no contact information. She clicked on the link titled "recent post" and groaned. A photo of her academy filled the screen. Piper read the headline out loud, "***Another murder at Haydn Music Academy? Say it isn't so!***" She scanned the rest of the article, the pit in her stomach growing with each line she read.

Cranberry Harbor police responded to a call at the academy this afternoon. A report of multiple bodies and a blood

splattered room leads us to believe an investigation of the academy is past due. Perhaps we need to investigate the Haydns' activities behind closed doors. No one is safe until we know the truth. Lock your doors folks. There's a killer on the loose.

    The Cranberry Harbor Tattler

Her hand shook as she clicked off the post and closed her computer. "Ugh. How can this be happening again?" She drew the afghan around her shoulders and walked to the rounded window, scanning the road, watching for the chief's car. Cold radiated off the window and she placed her hand near the sill. *Add weatherizing these ancient windows to the list.*

Owning a historic Cranberry Harbor home was a dream come true. Piper loved her old house, but the Victorian painted lady required loads of repairs. She and Rosie had tackled the sticky job of removing decades of wallpaper layers and re-papering the turret last summer, and she'd addressed most of the safety issues before she had moved in. Every job on the to-do list would improve the appearance of her home, but the chores felt never-ending. Her father and brothers hated how slowly she worked through the remodel, concerned for her safety. But despite all the naysayers, Piper loved the formidable task of rehabbing her dream house. She patted the windowsill. "You're a beautiful house. Don't believe what everyone says." A smile crossed her lips, but her chest tightened. "Rosie should have been back by now."

Shuffling back and forth between the window and sofa, Piper wore a path in her area rug. She rubbed at the carpet with her foot to fluff the pile and moved to the living room, continuing to pace. She'd almost given up hope when a car door slammed in the driveway. Piper ran to the door, yanking it open.

"Rosie," she hollered into the face of Chief Maxwell. She stepped into the arctic air to peek around the chief. Rosie skipped up the stairs.

"I'm baack," she sang. "Miss me?"

"Yes, get in here out of the cold. Didn't mean to yell in your face, Chief Maxwell."

He nodded and stepped into Piper's entryway. "I'll leave you ladies to your evening plans in a moment. I need to remind you to stay out of the investigation, Miss Haydn." He pointed at Rosie. "You too."

Rosie saluted. "Yes, sir."

"Miss Haydn?"

Piper nodded. "Of course."

The chief looked back and forth between the women and narrowed his eyes. "You both promised not to get involved in the investigation last time."

"And the time before," Rosie said, her eyes sparkling.

"Neither one of you plans to keep your word, do you?" He stared, his face stern.

Rosie drew an "x" over her heart. "Promise," she said, but the twinkle in her eyes offered a clue to her lack of sincerity.

He shook his head. "I know you want to help, but letting us do our job is the only help we need. Understand?"

Piper stepped toward the officer, pulling the front door open. "Got it."

He stepped onto the porch and cold air swirled into Piper's entry, chilling her feet before she had time to shut the door behind him.

Rosie peeled off her coat and hung it on the hook. "He's nuts if he thinks I'm staying out of this. Let me get something hot to drink and I'll fill you in." She hurried to the kitchen, and Piper settled on the sofa.

"Hurry, the anticipation is killing me."

"Argh! Don't say 'kill'," Rosie called from the kitchen.

Piper smirked and curled her feet underneath her, wrapping the blanket around her shoulders.

"He lost his mind. As I predicted," Rosie said.

Piper groaned. "Start from the beginning."

Rosie sipped tea and settled in for a round of storytelling. "When Fergus opened the door, he growled at Will."

"Will?" Piper's eyebrow arched.

"He told us to call him by his name ages ago. You remember."

Piper narrowed her eyes. "So, Fergus growled. And...?"

"He said the nativity is priceless, the set is an important historical piece, and he's planning to hold the Haydn family accountable for their destruction."

"I knew he'd threaten me. But in all fairness, he donated the nativity to the city. Can he sue me? And why my family? They aren't responsible for what happens at the academy."

Rosie slurped her tea and frowned. "How am I supposed to know? Doesn't your dad have an attorney on speed dial? Call him."

"Lenny? Yeah, but he's expensive."

"Back to the story," Rosie said. "He kept mumbling something about treasure and said he should have ignored his wife's bequest because the lunkheads in this town always ruin everything."

"Man, why is he so bitter?"

"Beats me." Rosie sipped her tea. "Interesting tidbit, about his *wife* requesting he donate the figures to the city. What do you think?"

Piper watched snowflakes blowing outside the window and shivered. "I don't remember meeting her."

"Apparently, Mrs. Fergus didn't find everyone in Cranberry Harbor a lunkhead." Rosie giggled and stretched her yellow clad legs across the couch.

"Phew, I need my sun shades for those leggings, Rosie," Piper said.

Rosie nudged her friend with frozen toes. "You love my outfit and secretly hanker for a matching pair of these babies."

Piper smiled. "Hanker? Dream on, friend."

"What about writing our questions and the clues in a notebook again?" Rosie threw off the blanket and moved to the piano, digging through Piper's music bag.

"Don't mess up the order of my sheet music!"

"Yeah, yeah, Miss Julliard. I'll be careful." She dug out a pencil and ripped a sheet of paper from Piper's notebook, and rejoined her friend on the sofa. "Why does this have these lines all over it?" She wrinkled her nose and held the paper up.

"Manuscript paper."

"Ooh la la. Fancy. Are you writing music?" She licked the end of the pencil and waggled her eyebrows.

"Always. What clues should we document?"

Rosie tapped the pencil on her lips. "Don found the figures. Do you think he did it?"

Piper shook her head. "No way. I trust him completely."

"Hmm... what about Lisa? She has access to the keys. Do you trust her?"

"I do, Rosie. She's made amends, and she only got in trouble because of her circumstances. Besides, why in the world would she knock the nativity around and destroy it? Not like her at all."

"I agree. So far, we have Don finding the 'murder.'" She held her fingers up in air quotes. "Three figures missing." She looked up from the notebook and frowned. "Weird. Plus, they're too big to hide. Where would they go with them? Someone had to see something."

"Write everything and we can attempt to decipher the clues little by little. We'll work through the list. By the way, the blog already reported this mess."

"Grr. How do they know already?" Rosie tapped her phone and searched for the article. "I'll leave a comment and tell them off for nosing in people's business."

"Telling them off won't help. You know they'll dig in their heels. Plus, tidbits about my family are newsworthy in this town."

"Gossip isn't news," Rosie said, her eyes blazing.

"Let's not dwell on the blog. What else should we add to the notebook?"

Rosie tapped the pencil on the paper and stared out the window. "Does the weather have anything to do with this?"

"I don't see how, but add weather to the list. You never know how clues might come together to solve the puzzle later. Did Fergus say what country the nativity set came from?"

"Nope. Do you remember anything from the ceremony last year when they acknowledged the donation?"

Piper searched her memory. "No, if I remember correctly, I was at the other end of the park, lining up our carolers from the academy to sing after the Christmas tree lighting." She snapped her fingers. "Speaking of caroling, I hope this arctic weather warms up or we'll be popsicles out there."

Piper searched for the weather forecast and read aloud. "Report says warming to the low to mid-twenties by Saturday."

"We can handle the low twenties. Wisconsin folks are hearty, but I'll need to wear a double layer of leggings." Rosie giggled.

"Can you at least try to wear Christmas colors for caroling?"

"Hey," Rosie said, and pouted. "The star over the manger was yellow. I'm being spiritual." She stretched. "I need to get home. My kitties are probably ready to call the humane society for animal neglect. I need to turn the faucets on to drip to keep the pipes from freezing. You better do the same."

"Goodness, I didn't even think of the pipes freezing. Exactly what this old house needs." She groaned. "Call me when you get home, so I know you're safe."

Rosie squeezed Piper's shoulders and blew a kiss. "Of course I will. What are you doing the rest of the night? I'm painting labels for the Christkindlmarket and then I'm curling up in my bed to catch up on all the T.V. shows I've missed."

"Reading and fretting over this fiasco."

Rosie shook her finger at Piper. "Isn't worry a sin? Everything will work out the way it's supposed to. And hey, at least it's not actually a murder this time."

Piper shuddered. "Thank God."

"Night," Rosie called.

Piper watched for a moment. Her friend's words echoing. No. This wasn't murder, but the unease swirling in her brain and the pit in her stomach knocked her off balance.

She sat at the piano, resting her fingers on the smooth keys. Piper closed her eyes and played the chorus of her favorite Christmas piece, "Still, Still, Still." She whispered the lyrics as her hands moved over the piano. "All is hushed. The world is sleeping. Holy Star its vigil keeping..." The melody swirled around her as she trailed off, praying for the music to soothe her soul.

CHAPTER 2

Friday

The phone on her nightstand chirped, waking Piper from a fitful sleep. She had tossed and turned all night, her mind racing with questions. She rubbed her eyes and yawned, tapping the phone to stop the alarm. Stars twinkled in the dusky sky, but sun rays peeked through thin clouds. Because of the deep freeze, Cranberry Harbor schools had closed the past two days. To protect her students and teachers, she followed their lead and closed the Haydn Music Academy.

"No need to get out of bed," she whispered, nestling beneath the cozy quilt. Her mind battled between her to-do list and her desire to curl up under the blankets and snooze. She groaned and jumped up, quickly spreading her blankets across the bed and smoothing wrinkles to fight her temptation.

On her way downstairs, the squeaky step creaked, echoing in the quiet house. Rosie was right. Her noisy tread was an excellent security system. *Maybe I should leave it—adds character.* She adjusted the thermostat to raise the temperature in the chilly house and started a pot of coffee.

While her morning caffeine brewed, she read the weather report and smiled. "Already ten degrees warmer and the sun hasn't even risen." She breathed a sigh of relief and poured coffee into a mug before settling on the couch in the turret.

The sheet of manuscript paper on the side table reminded her of the damaged nativity set and all the commotion yesterday. She frowned and picked up the paper and a pen. She sipped coffee as she read the list Rosie had scribbled last night. Stray thoughts and threads of ideas pinged through her mind, unsettling her.

She scribbled Fergus' name and then erased it. Sunshine rose above the trees, filling her room with light and lifting her spirits. Tossing aside the paper, she opened her notepad and checked her to-do list for the day. She drew a line through the tree lighting ceremony and Caroling Extravaganza. The parks department had the tree standing in the park ready for the mayor to plug in the strand of lights. Everyone would "ooh" and "ah" and then townspeople would gather in their caroling groups and travel through Cranberry Harbor, spreading Christmas cheer.

Piper read her notes and reviewed the groups she'd created. Eight people had volunteered to lead, and she had given each group several stops around town. Lisa had copied the lyrics onto sheets and stapled pages into small song books. Rosie's hand drawn picture of carolers decorated the covers and the songbooks waited at the academy ready to go.

Downtown businesses planned to open for the extra traffic. Cafes and restaurants would serve complimentary hot drinks and light snacks to keep everyone's energy from flagging. If the weather cooperated, they'd sail through the evening, creating memories and brightening the season for lonely citizens. Piper scanned the list once more, satisfied she had covered all the bases. Nothing could go wrong other than someone slipping on the ice or croaking Christmas carols out of tune, but Piper wouldn't stress. Most of the people receiving carolers wouldn't cringe at off-key singing. She had, however, assigned the discordant voices to other groups to protect her ears from agony all evening. Piper smiled at her little organizational trick, but felt slightly guilty when she read the list of people she'd assigned to the other groups.

"Forgive me, Lord," she whispered. "But my ears can't handle too much 'joyful noise' in one evening."

Her phone rang, interrupting her irreverent prayer.

"Hello, Miss Haydn. Chief Maxwell here. I have a few questions if you have time?"

"Sure. Do you want me to come to the station?"

"No, but can I swing by in thirty minutes?"

She tied the belt of her scruffy robe and cleared her throat. "Umm, sure. Make it forty-five?"

"See you then." He hung up, and Piper jumped from the couch to dress before he arrived.

Half an hour later, Piper headed downstairs in her piano teacher uniform—navy blue pencil skirt, white blouse, pink floral voile scarf, and pink ballerina flats. She tugged a brush through her snarled hair and twisted it into a ponytail, tucking the ends under to create a messy bun. Excitement bubbled, and she scolded herself. *Stop it. He's on police business investigating the break-in.* She'd told everyone around town she was too busy to date and emphasized her disinterest in the police chief. But her flip-flopping heart betrayed her. *Thank God Rosie isn't here. She'd never let me live this down.*

Piper refilled the teakettle and turned on the flame. Keeping busy might calm her nerves and stop her from acting a fool in front of the chief. She rested her hand on her heart and inhaled, closing her eyes. "Knock it off, Piper," she said out loud. "You're going to embarrass yourself."

When the doorbell chimed, Piper hurried to the front to greet the police chief, but found Rosie peering through the window, smiling.

"You're all dressed up for a snow day. What's up?" Rosie hung her coat on the hook.

Piper pointed at Rosie. "What's up with me? What's up with your sweater? The 90s are calling and they want their ugly sweater back."

"Hey," Rosie said, turning in circles. "Don't insult the Christmas sweater. I wore green leggings today to make you happy."

Piper laughed. "Lime green."

"Green is green, my friend. Back to my question. Why are you up and at 'em, all dressed up so early on a snow day?" A shadow fell across the entryway and Rosie turned. "Oh," she said and whistled. She turned her back to the window and winked at Piper. "And all the clues fall into place. Just...like... that." She snapped her fingers and grinned.

Piper reached around her friend and opened the door for the police chief.

"Good morning, ladies. I didn't expect to find you here so early, Rosie, but I'm glad. I have a few more questions for you as well." He followed Piper into the living room and pulled out his notebook. "Miss Haydn, do you have security cameras at the academy?"

"Yes, but I'm afraid they won't be of any use." Her cheeks reddened. "Last week, the batteries died, and I completely forgot to remind Don to replace them. I meant to, but I didn't write a note on my list and I didn't think anything would happen."

"Can you turn over whatever recordings you have? Perhaps the break-in happened before Don's discovery yesterday."

"Interesting thought," Rosie said. "Technically, those creeps could have broken in any time since last Christmas and yesterday, right?"

"Technically, yes, but I didn't notice dust on the debris. They haven't been lying in the storeroom in this condition for very long."

His attention shifted to Piper. "Have you noticed anyone hanging around? Someone coming in too often? Angry parents?"

Piper considered his question. "I don't remember, but I'm not in the office as often as Lisa is."

"I'll talk to her. How can I get the security recordings? Can an employee meet one of my officers at your academy this afternoon?"

Piper nodded. "Should I talk to Lisa?"

"Yes, please. Call me either way. Now, Miss Hale, how long have you worked for Fergus?"

"Less than six months. And I haven't noticed any shifty characters hanging around his place either. Is anyone mad at Fergus? Can't say. But we all know Fergus hates the whole town."

Chief Maxwell smiled. "I noticed. Did you notice anything out of the ordinary in his home?"

Rosie blushed.

Chief Maxwell crossed his arms. "Miss Hale?"

"She snoops through his drawers when she dusts," Piper tattled.

"It's not snooping. I'm doing a thorough job and getting dust out of the inside of his drawers, too. I can't help what I see while I'm cleaning."

The chief rubbed his mouth, hiding a smirk, and cleared his throat. "Have you seen anything of interest when you dust inside his drawers?"

Rosie crossed her arms and squinted her eyes. "Don't you need a warrant or something for these questions? If I tell you what I saw and you don't have a warrant, it might blow the whole case apart."

He stared. "Too many nighttime crime shows, huh?"

"I try to stay informed. Got a problem?" She narrowed her eyes and tossed her hair. Her jingle bell earrings tinkling as she moved.

"Of course not, but they aren't accurate. Back to my question..." He tapped the notebook with his pencil and checked his watch.

"Nothing too exciting. In Mrs. Standerwick's room, I saw a lot of books and letters in German. At least I think it's German. But nothing else I can think of. Too bad he didn't give you a tour of his house. The place is magnificent."

"I'm not interested in his house other than any clues we might find to help us figure out who destroyed the nativity."

"He can't sue Piper, can he?" Rosie asked.

"She needs to consult an attorney. Not a question I can answer."

"What do you need?" Piper asked.

"I'll collect your security recordings, talk to Lisa, and go from there. If you don't mind, I'm sending a couple of officers back to the storage room to take another look. What time can they stop?"

"Two o'clock? I'll have the recordings ready."

"See you then. Thank you." He buttoned his jacket, and Piper rose to walk him out.

"Sounds like a date to me," Rosie said.

Piper turned and glared at Rosie, but Chief Maxwell grinned.

"By the way, ladies, I'm serious about you staying out of the investigation."

Piper bit her tongue, unwilling to lie.

He moved his head up and down. "Copy me. Nod your head and say, 'I understand.'"

Rosie clapped her hands and giggled. "With all due respect, sir, you know we can't promise."

Chief Maxwell stepped to the door. "Will you at least let me know if you come across any clues?"

"Of course. If we find details you need to know, we'll tell you," Piper said.

"Toodles," Rosie said as the chief left.

"He's infuriating," Piper said, turning away from the door.

Rosie grinned.

"What?"

Rosie smiled and hummed "Unforgettable".

"Please don't tease, Rosie."

Rosie squeezed Piper and kissed her cheek. "Why don't you give him a chance? I know you like him."

Piper stepped back. "Your sweater is scratchy." She marched to the turret and held out the sheet of paper. "Now, about these clues."

"Are you trying to change the subject, Miss Haydn?" Rosie frowned.

"Exactly. The clues." She pointed to the paper.

Rosie plopped onto the sofa. "Alright. Hit me with them. Refresh my mind."

Piper read the clues they'd written last night, and Rosie closed her eyes. She popped one eye open. "Wait. Read through them again." She tapped her finger to her lips and frowned. "Are you sure you don't think Don had *anything* to do with this?"

"What is bothering you about Don?"

"He was the only one there. What if he damaged the pieces, hid the three he wanted, and reported a break-in?"

"Rosie, you know Don. You've watched his kids and hung out with his wife. Really?"

Rosie blew out a breath. "You're right." She reached for her phone. "Let me read the dumb blog again."

Piper's phone rang, and she tapped the speakerphone so Rosie could listen in. "Chase, what's up?"

"I read the Tattler. Miss Perfect Piper finds herself in another scrape." He hooted. "What did you do this time?"

"Someone broke in and destroyed the nativity set and three pieces are missing."

Chase whistled. "The set Fergus donated? Oh, boy."

"Exactly."

"Where were they?"

"In the storage room, way down the back hallway."

The other end of the line was silent.

"Chase?"

Chase cleared his throat. "I gotta go." The call disconnected, and Piper stared at her phone.

Rosie scribbled across the paper. "Chase Haydn acting weird. Clue number five." She stopped and erased her clue. "On the other hand, when doesn't Chase Haydn act weird?" She stuck out her tongue and Piper tossed a pillow at her.

"Be nice to my brother, Roosevelt." She stared out the window. "You know what? Write his name on the list. He's acting very strange."

Rosie folded the paper and tucked it into the pocket on the chest of her massive Christmas sweater. "Let's swing by Dominique's before we pull up your security recordings."

"Excellent idea. I want to talk with her about the Christkindlmarket, anyway." She smoothed the afghan over the back of the couch and reached for the pillow she'd tossed at Rosie.

"Rosie, should I call Chase back? Something seems off." She frowned.

"I already mentioned Chase acting like Chase is normal. Didn't seem any different than his usual weird self."

"Maybe. I'll call Lisa before we leave. Give me a minute."

"I'll warm up my car."

Warm, spicy air greeted them when Rosie opened the bakery door. "Mmm. What are we baking at Sweetberry's today, Mrs. Landry?" she called.

Dominique stepped out of the kitchen, wiping her hands on a red and green apron. White streaks of flour scattered across her brown arms and sprinkled to the floor when she reached to hug Piper. "What are my babies doing out on such a cold day?" She smiled at Rosie and kissed her cheek, leaving a dusting of flour on her Christmas sweater.

Rosie brushed the flour from her sweater and blew a kiss to Dominique. "We wanted to investigate the delicious smells wafting from your bakery."

Dominique chuckled. "Are you telling me the delicious smells from my bakery wafted clear across town?"

"Subliminally. I knew you were baking yummy stuff today. What did ya make?"

Dominique moved back to the kitchen and motioned for the girls to follow. Trays of gingerbread cookies covered every surface in the room.

"Rosie wonders what you're baking today, and I'm curious about your Christkindlmarket plans."

Dominique pointed around the room. "You're looking at it."

"Gingerbread men?" Rosie squealed, leaning in to inhale the aroma.

"Today is batch number four. I've tweaked several recipes and I think this might be the one. Here." She handed each of them a gingerbread man cookie the size of a dinner plate.

Rosie snapped the head off of hers and ate it in one bite.

Dominique stared at her with wide eyes. "Brutal, honey."

Rosie giggled and stuffed an arm in her mouth. "I always bite the head off first. Don't you?"

Dominique shook her head. "Mercy, girl." She pulled another tray of cookies from the oven. Cloves, cinnamon, and ginger filled the air. "I'm tryin' to decide if I'll sell them decorated, or set up a decorating station. What do you think?"

"Both," Rosie said around a mouthful of gingerbread cookie. She swallowed. "Decorated cookies for parents who don't want to wait in line with whiny children and a decoration station for anyone with patience."

Dominque blew a kiss in Rosie's direction. "Brilliant. Do you approve, Piper?"

"Of course. Are all your cookies going to be this huge?"

"The bigger, the better when we're talking about gingerbread cookies, my dear."

Piper munched on her treat. "These are delicious. I think you're right. The recipe is perfect."

"Wait 'til you try them with icing and cinnamon red hots for buttons."

"We used to make gingerbread cookies when I was a kid," Rosie said. "My brothers spread icing all over the kitchen and Mom hollered at them."

"And you," Dominque pointed at Rosie. "You decapitated their heads and devoured them."

"Bingo," Rosie said and snapped the head off another cookie.

Dominique swatted Rosie's hands away from the cookies. "You can't eat all of them today. You're hurting my profits."

"Oops," Rosie mumbled around the cookie in her mouth.

"Piper," Dominique frowned, "I read the blog. What's happening, precious? Why does a sweet girl like you keep running into these scrapes?"

"I can't explain it, Mrs. Landry, but at least this time there's no murder."

"Until Fergus finds out."

"He already knows," Rosie said.

"And?"

"He's hopping mad. He claims the town is filled with lunkheads and regrets donating the nativity. Oh, and he's suing the Haydns."

Dominique snorted. "Good grief. What do you think happened, Piper?"

Piper's smile faded. "I'm not sure, Dominique. We're heading over to pull up security recordings, but I don't think we'll find anything. The batteries ran out, and I forgot to ask Don to replace them."

"Rotten timing there, lamb." Dominique held a thick wooden rolling pin and pinched a ball of brown fragrant dough from a gigantic metal mixing bowl. "I need to get these cookies baked and in the freezer. I'll say a prayer for you, baby. Keep the faith and don't trouble yourself over Fergus. I'll whack him with my rolling pin if necessary." She laughed and shifted to her butcher block counter, her strong arms flying as she moved the rolling pin back and forth. "Let me know if you find anything on those recordings."

"You'll let us know if you hear anything?"

"Absolutely. You two button up before you go out. We don't need you catching cold on top of everything else. I'll see you at caroling tomorrow night." She hummed the *Hallelujah Chorus* while rolling gingerbread dough, then waved a floury hand as the girls left.

Piper smiled at Cranberry Harbor's charming Main Street. Wreaths hung from each light post, with white lights strung between them. At night, you might mistake downtown Cranberry Harbor for the set of a magical Christmas movie. Every store on Main Street displayed a 1960s aluminum Christmas tree decorated with vintage ornaments and surrounded by Christmas props. Tourists from all over Wisconsin came to enjoy the vintage atomic trees. The chamber of commerce would judge the windows and give out prizes on the final evening of the Christkindlmarket.

"Is everything ready for caroling tomorrow night?" Rosie asked as they settled into her car.

"Thanks to Lisa, caroling is under control."

"I'm glad things worked out with her. You know. After everything," Rosie said.

"Me too, friend."

Lisa waited at the door of the academy. "What's going on?"

"Someone stole three of the nativity scene figures and destroyed the other pieces," Piper said.

"Oh no. Fergus is going to lose his mind." Lisa gasped.

"Too late. Already happened," Rosie said.

Lisa's eyes widened. "Why are we meeting the police?"

"An officer is stopping by to pick up the security footage and Chief Maxwell has questions for you," Piper said.

"Wait a minute." Lisa looked back and forth between Rosie and Piper. "You don't suspect me, do you?" Tears filled her eyes.

Piper put an arm around her. "No. No one suspects you. Only some questions."

Rosie patted Lisa's arm. "Cheer up, friend. Only a police interrogation."

"Rosie!" both women said in unison and Rosie giggled, running down the hall, flipping the lights on as she went.

"What do you want me to do?" Lisa asked.

"When we get to the office, I need you to download security footage while we wait for the officers."

Lisa squared her shoulders. "I can handle that," she said, but her hands trembled.

"Take a deep breath. Everything is fine." Piper smiled as they stepped into her office. Rosie sat in Piper's desk chair, spinning in circles and laughing. Her jingle bell earrings ringing a merry tune as she twirled.

Piper checked the key rack near the door. Had someone moved the storage room keys? She couldn't remember. She wasn't picky about where the keys hung as long as her staff had access. But today the set of keys dangled on the hook, hanging from a hole in one key instead of hanging from the ring. She stepped to the wall and tugged the key wedged onto the hook and flipped through the ring. Nothing seemed amiss.

"You can start downloading the recordings while we wait," she said to her secretary.

Lisa logged into her computer, and Rosie spun the chair at Piper's desk, shouting out questions every time she faced Piper.

"Isn't the whole thing so weird?" Spin. Jingle. Giggle. "Who in the world did it?" Spin. Jingle. Giggle. "Wouldn't it be something if Fergus did it?" Spin.

"Rosie! You're making me dizzy," Piper said.

Rosie planted her feet on the floor to stop the chair from spinning. "I beg your forgiveness." She propped her elbows on Piper's desk and winked.

Piper moved to stand behind Lisa, watching while her secretary downloaded the security footage.

Rosie joined the women at Lisa's desk and watched her scroll through several days of recordings. When two figures appeared in one frame, all three women stared at the computer, then at each other.

"Who...? Is that...?" Rosie asked, pointing at one of the figures.

"Can't tell for sure. Picture's grainy," Lisa said.

Piper nodded and gulped. "Rewind."

Lisa scrolled backwards on the video and took a deep breath. She hit pause and cleared her throat.

Piper clenched her teeth.

"Chase," Rosie whispered. Her cheerful smile disappeared, and tears gathered in the corners of her eyes. "What's he doing in the alley?"

"Want me to delete this?" Lisa tapped the screen.

Piper stared for a moment, her conscience warring. She reached her hand out and hovered over the delete key, but snatched it back. "No. The protective sister in me wants to hit delete, but we can't."

"We don't need to tell the police, though," Rosie said. "They can find it themselves. Give Piper time to talk to Chase."

"Or beat some sense into him," she said.

"Good idea." Rosie patted Piper. "Everything will work out."

Piper rested her hand on Rosie's arm. "Thank you. Thank you, too, Lisa."

The office phone rang, and Lisa answered. "Haydn Music Academy, this is Lisa. How may I help you?" she said, placing her hands over the speaker and mouthing, "police".

Rosie bounded into the hall. "I'll let them in," she hollered and disappeared.

In the early evening, Piper curled up on the sofa and stretched. Rosie had dropped her off and headed home after the long day at the academy. Answering police questions and waiting around for the officers to finish searching the storage room had drained her energy. Her feet ached and unpleasant questions about her brother's presence in the alley behind the school plagued her.

Tomorrow's Caroling Extravaganza needed her attention right now. She planned to review the list of details and check it twice. She read her scribbled notes and dropped the list on the floor. Picking up her phone, she punched in Chase's number.

"Hey, Piper."

"Chase Haydn. Help me understand something."

His silence hung in the air, and Piper's chest tightened. "Chase?"

"Yeah," he said, his usual cockiness missing.

"Why did you hang up this morning?" she demanded.

"Listen, I'm busy here."

"Busy? What are you busy with, Chase? I am running a Christmas market, organizing the town caroling event, directing the community choir's production of Handel's *Messiah*, running my business, and now fielding questions from the police over missing nativity figures."

"Yeah, I know. Cranberry Harbor wouldn't survive without Piper the Perfect."

"Chase."

"Whatever, I gotta go."

"Chase, why were you loitering in the alley behind the academy with a stranger the other day?"

Chase cleared his throat. "What are you talking about?"

"You know exactly what I'm talking about. I can hear it in your voice. I suggest you show up at my home in ten minutes and explain to me what's going on."

"Or what?"

"Or what? Really, Chase? Are you ten years old? Or else, I'll make sure Chief Maxwell notices the exact time you were loitering in my alley with a stranger right before the figures went missing."

"Come on, Piper. You'd never report me."

"The police already have the footage, Chase. They'll find you on it before long. I hoped you'd come clean. Help me understand why you're in a mess again.

"Fine. I'm on my way."

Piper dropped her phone and stared out the window. Darkness seeped through the windowpanes, but a glimmer of moonlight shone across the piano. "I could use some help here, Lord. Why is Chase always getting caught up in trouble? I love my brother, but he needs help."

She picked up her book and flipped through the pages, but couldn't concentrate. She tossed it onto the couch and moved to the piano. The cool keys seemed to whisper, "Everything's going to work out fine." She stretched her fingers and laid her hands on the keyboard to play, pouring her pent up stress into pounding out the "Hallelujah Chorus". Her fingers stretched, easily moving through the melismas and trills. The knots in her neck loosened, and the heaviness she'd held in her heart slipped away as she lost herself in the majestic melody. Her eyes closed, and she swayed gently as she played. When she reached the end of the piece, music had worked the magic it always worked in her soul. Peace and joy flooded her spirit. She slid the lid over the piano keys and gasped when she turned from the piano.

"Chase. Why didn't you knock? You scared me half to death."

Chase stared. "Door was open. What do you want?"

"Come here." She opened the email Lisa had sent with the security footage. After several moments of scrolling, she turned the screen to her brother and lowered her voice. "Well?"

Chase held up his hands. "This is not what it looks like. I can explain."

Piper crossed her arms and stared.

"Can I sit?" Chase moved to the couch and tugged off his jacket.

Piper tapped her watch and cleared her throat.

"I'm getting there," he said, narrowing his eyes. He rested his elbows on his knees and rubbed his hands together. "You have anything hot to drink?"

"Chase!"

"Alright. Several days ago, I jogged past your academy during my morning run, and some old lady stopped me. She wanted to know what was going on in there. I told her my sister owned the building now, and it's a music academy. She told me some long story about going to school there back in the day. Her mom taught art and her dad was the principal."

"Did she say her name?"

Chase shook his head. "I have no idea who she is. I never saw her before or since."

"Why were you in the alley with her?"

He held up his hand and glared. "I'm getting to it. Hold your horses."

Piper narrowed her eyes. "Chase Haydn."

He frowned. "She told me she and her friends used to sneak in and out the back way and wanted to find out if the door was still there. I wasn't trying to hang out with her. She basically dragged me to the alley."

"What door was she talking about?"

"The big one way around the back, but I couldn't open it. Probably locked." Chase rubbed his hands together. "I hoped she'd move on, but she wanted a tour for old times' sake. I found Lisa's car parked in the lot, so I left the woman in the alley and went to see what your secretary thought of the idea. When I found Lisa, we walked to the office for the keys, but the ring was missing. She said her coffee was brewing and I could wait there or walk with her to collect her coffee mug. I followed and grabbed a cup of coffee to take along. We found the keys hanging on the hook when we returned to the office. Lisa laughed and said something about her lack of coffee. I went to find the old lady in the alley, but she had disappeared. So I left."

Piper frowned. "You didn't think any of this was odd?"

"Yeah. The whole thing was weird, but I didn't do anything, Piper, so don't accuse me."

"Why didn't you tell me?"

"Because I don't call you about every little thing. You're not my mother, and frankly, I'm tired of being accused of every crime in this town."

Piper crossed her arms and bit her tongue before she said something she'd regret. "In the future, Chase, when something odd happens at my academy, I'd like to know. Suppose she's a creep and attempting to gather information about one of my students or teachers?"

"Come on, now you're stretching things. You think weird stuff happens around here? Good grief. She could barely keep up with me. I sincerely doubt she's a threat to anyone."

"Deciding who's a threat is up to me, Chase, not you. I have to consider the safety of my students."

"Blah blah blah," Chase said, holding his hand as if he moved a puppet's mouth.

Piper's eyes widened. "My goodness, Chase. I think you should go home now, but I suggest you prepare a better story before the police question you. No one will fall for this crazy little tale you spun."

Her brother jumped up, shoving past her. He slammed her front door, rattling the glass.

Piper gritted her teeth and dropped onto the piano bench, flipping the lid open. Her fingers pounded out section three from Handel's *Messiah* and hummed along with the melody, mouthing the words. "If God be for us, who can be against us?" The confusion and fear she'd carried since Don's call melted as her fingers moved over the keys. Concern for Chase and the nativity set and the unknown criminal bounced through her thoughts. "Hey, God," she whispered as she played. "Can you help me carry these burdens? Help me lay this mess down and trust you to work all things for good."

She rose from the piano, flipped off the lights, double checked the lock on the front door, and climbed the stairs. One of the squeaky steps creaked when she stepped on the tread, and Rosie's idea to keep it for a security system struck her as brilliant. Should she fear an intruder? Probably not, but something felt odd about the break-in at the academy, and she struggled to maintain peace.

Piper slipped under the quilt and watched the stars outside her windowpane. Tomorrow, they'd go caroling and spread cheer through the town. Tonight, she'd sleep and soon everything would return to normal and the citizens of Cranberry Harbor would celebrate Christmas in peace.

Piper closed her eyes. "Nothing to worry about," she whispered, turning over and drifting to sleep.

Chapter 3

Holy star, its vigil keeping.

Saturday Morning

Sun streamed through Piper's window. She squinted, wrapping the quilt around her shoulders and ignoring the beeping alarm. The Caroling Extravaganza tonight promised to keep her running until bedtime, and she groaned, thinking of the fractured nativity scene. Her conversation with Chase last night rumbled in her mind. From his version of events, he appeared innocent. But why the defensiveness?

Her phone rang, and she rolled over to answer.

"You up?" Rosie's voice, too chipper for morning filled her room.

"No, but I'm working on it."

"Well, hurry down and open your door. I'm on the way over with a massive latte from Ruby's. I ordered you the Christmas spice latte with two extra shots of espresso."

Piper laughed. "Thanks. Caffeine might keep me moving all day. I'll let you in." On her way, she cranked up the thermostat and unlocked the door as Rosie arrived.

She hopped out of her car holding a drink carrier and held up a bag. "Stopped at Sweetberry's too. Dominique texted me to come taste test her chocolate cranberry pie." Rosie giggled. "I'm not touching the pie, because you know, chocolate. But I couldn't resist a cranberry cinnamon roll. Here, take something." She held out the food to Piper and breezed into the house. Rosie pulled her arms out of her heavy coat and twirled. "How's this outfit for caroling?" She wore a white A-line jumper, green tights, a red and white striped turtleneck and poinsettia earrings the size of sugar cookies.

"You're a Christmas carol in the flesh," Piper said, hugging her friend.

"Oh, good, because Lincoln saw me at Ruby's and said I resembled a frightening elf."

Piper rolled her eyes. "Brothers."

"Speaking of brothers, did you talk to Chase?" She grabbed the bag and handed Piper a to-go box and a plastic fork.

"Let's use plates. Dominique's food is too good to eat from to-go boxes." In the kitchen, Piper pulled bright red Waechtersbach Christmas plates from the cupboard.

"Ooh la la. Fancy," Rosie said, running her fingers across the green tree on the earthenware plate. "Where'd you get these?"

"Mom started collecting these for me when I was small. Our grandma had this set, and I loved the dishes so much. Mom's Christmas dishes are Spode and much daintier, but I love these. Makes me feel like Grandma is still here."

Rosie smiled. "They make me smile too. We never had Christmas dishes—or matching dishes."

"I'm sorry."

Rosie smiled. "Oh, it's fine. Life got hard when Dad left, but Mom did great. She didn't have extra money for fancy things, but she did a good job with us."

"I own way too many Christmas dishes. Pick out a few to take home. Here." She handed Rosie a red soup bowl decorated with green trees.

Rosie's eyes sparkled. "Really? You know, I'm not broke anymore—thanks to my excellent boss at the Haydn Music Academy. I can hunt for my own Christmas dishes."

Piper patted Rosie's back. "Of course you can purchase your own dishes, but when you take mine, you'll think of me while enjoying Christmas treats."

"You twisted my arm. Now, back to Chase."

Piper sighed. "I told him to come over last night. Basically, he spun a yarn about meeting some old lady while he was running past the academy and she begged him to show her around the school for old times' sake. But she disappeared before he had a chance."

Rosie raised an eyebrow. "Good grief. What a tall tale."

"He also said he's sick of everyone accusing him and stormed out, slamming my front door. I thought he was going to break the windowpane."

"We don't think Chase destroyed the figures or hid anything, do we? Where's our clues sheet?"

Piper handed Rosie a fresh notebook. "Start over. We'll end up losing this sheet of paper."

"No to Don," Rosie said, writing as she spoke. "No to Lisa. Maybe to Chase, but what did he supposedly do? What are we missing?"

Piper pointed her fork at Rosie. "I can't do detective work right now. This heavenly pie needs all my concentration." She dug into the silky chocolate and closed her eyes. "Mmm. Is this a gingerbread crust? Dominique hit it out of the ballpark with this recipe."

Rosie pinched off the edges of her cinnamon roll and nodded. "She's a treasure. Back to the topic."

"I can't make sense of it. Destroying the nativity seems pointless. Can you imagine a random old woman hacking apart a nativity scene?"

"Who knows? Oh. I'll tell you something odd. My phone rang early this morning and Fergus' name lit up the screen, but when I answered, he wasn't there."

"Has he accidentally called before?"

Rosie tapped the pencil on the notebook and stared out the window. "Maybe? When I first started and he wanted me to work at a different time. I can't remember."

"Probably nothing. When are you supposed to work next?"

"Not 'til after New Year. Remember? His sister-in-law is coming to visit."

"Right. I wouldn't worry. He probably dialed you by mistake."

"Anything new on the blog?" Rosie snapped and pointed at Piper. "Hey! What if the person vandalizing the nativity set is also the one writing the Tattler?"

"Unlikely, don't you think?" Piper opened the internet on her phone and typed in 'Cranberry Harbor Tattler'.

Rosie hovered over her shoulder and groaned. She read aloud.

"Cranberry Harbor's Christmas ruined. Antique nativity set destroyed while in possession of the Haydn family. How the Haydn family came to have possession of this historic set remains a question we'd like answered. The set belongs to the city, and yet the most powerful family in town commandeered and destroyed the antique pieces to keep everyone else from enjoying them. The authorities have not provided the public with evidence of the destruction. Perhaps the Haydn family sold the antiques and staged a break-in? This situation is developing. We will update as details become available."
The Cranberry Harbor Tattler

Rosie scowled. "Are you kidding me? I oughta…"

"Easy, girl," Piper said. "The police know the details. Let's ignore this." She clicked off the article and pressed play on her Handel playlist.

"Handel's the composer of choice this season?" Rosie asked.

"Yep. Immersing myself in Baroque. Between leading the community choir production of the *Messiah*, and singing the "Hallelujah Chorus" in the church choir, my life is all Handel all the time."

"I like good old George," Rosie said with a grin.

The soaring music filled Piper's kitchen while they munched their morning sweets. Rosie tapped her toes to the beat and Piper hummed the measures she had memorized.

Rosie licked her fingertips and jumped from the kitchen stool. "When are we decorating this Victorian showplace for Christmas?"

Piper groaned. "Umm…maybe in my spare time? The Christkindlmarket and community choir take up every moment."

"You simply must decorate a tree to display in the turret window, Piper Haydn."

"Why?"

"One, because everyone adores driving past these old ladies and seeing lit trees in the windows. Nostalgia, I tell you. They want to dream of past Christmases celebrated in these grand old homes. Two, because I want to plop on your couch every day and stare at the beauty."

"Well, then I'll figure something out."

Rosie blew an air kiss and licked the last of the icing from her fingers. "What are you wearing for the Caroling Extravaganza?"

"I haven't decided. Something warm."

"Something warm and cute." She smiled and fluttered her eyelashes. "Chief Maxwell will be there."

Piper gathered the red dishes and wiped the counter. "Oh brother."

"What?"

"I'm not dressing to impress Chief Maxwell."

"I think he likes you," Rosie teased.

"Enough, Roosevelt. Stop teasing me and help me pick out my outfit for tonight."

Rosie skipped up the old staircase. "Whoa, this one really *is* creaky. I like it. Gives the house character."

"What would I do without you?" Piper smiled.

"You'd wear black or white every day and live a very boring existence."

Rosie rummaged through Piper's closet, tossing clothes on the bed.

Piper crossed her arms as the pile grew. "Who's hanging all these clothes up when we're done?"

"I'm not the maid. I'm your stylist. Here, try this."

Several moments later, Piper stood in front of the mirror, smiling. Rosie had talked her into wearing far more color than she preferred, but the pieces went together nicely, especially for a Christmas caroling party.

"Take a twirl," Rosie said, and Piper obeyed.

Piper wore a pair of pink pants, a mint green top, a white cable-knit sweater, with a red and white candy striped scarf. Pale pink earrings and a forest green scarf pulled through her belt loops completed the look. "Non-traditional, but I like it."

Rosie bowed low to the ground. "At your service, madam."

Piper checked the time. "We have a couple of hours before the caroling chaos begins. I think we should sneak over to the academy and examine those destroyed figures. Are you coming with me?"

"It's like you don't even know me. Of course I'm coming. What about the chief?"

Piper tilted her head and rested her hands on her hips. "Did worrying about the chief ever stop us before?"

Rosie giggled. "I'll bring the notebook to document all the clues we're gonna find. Let's go, Nancy Drew."

Piper and Rosie entered the Haydn Music Academy through a back door. "Why do I feel like we're trespassing?" Piper asked.

"Because Chief Maxwell would throw a fit if he knew we were doing this."

"I guess I can walk around my own property." She stopped. "Hey, don't turn on the lights. I don't want to get caught."

Rosie giggled. "Sure, Miss I Can Walk Around My Own Property. No lights. Got it." She skipped down the hallway, humming a tune.

"Tell me you're not humming country music in my academy. Roosevelt?"

A giggle filled the hallway. "I'll never tell." She waited for Piper at the storage room door, and they stood in silence for a moment. "Well, are you going to open the door?"

Piper tugged the key from her Chanel bag and Rosie tapped the flashlight button on her phone. They tiptoed into the pitch-black storage room.

"A selfie of us right about now would make an excellent book cover for a mystery," Rosie said.

"Shh."

"Why are we whispering?"

"I don't know," Piper said. "I have a weird feeling."

Rosie bolted past Piper and stopped in front of the damaged nativity scene. She counted out loud. "Eleven, twelve, thirteen... yep. Three pieces missing."

"Well, who would have broken into my storage room and put the pieces back?"

"You never know about criminals. They don't think like the rest of us," Rosie said, tapping her forehead.

"True," Piper said and knelt before the figures. She ran her fingers over the shepherd. Paint chips fell from the jagged break at his neck. She brushed the chips from her pants. Her eyes moved over the figure and she reached for the donkey. "Poor guy lost his ears," she said. "Shine the flashlight over here, please?"

Rosie stepped behind Piper and shone the light into the hollow shepherd. She leaned down, collecting the shepherd's head from the floor and handing it to Piper. "See anything?"

Piper ran her hands over the face and shuddered. "Creepy. Feels like he's staring at me." She rested the head next to the body and stood. "Let's get a better look inside."

Rosie held her phone over the broken shepherd and they peered inside the opening. "I don't see anything. You?"

"No. He's empty. I can't tell if this is plaster or wood?"

Rosie stepped to the shepherd and ran her fingers over the surface, peering inside the body. "Wood for sure. With the hit this poor guy took, he'd turn to dust if made from plaster."

"What are we searching for?" Piper ran her hands over the figure.

"Whatever it takes to explain this fiasco." Rosie leaned over and peered into the donkey, but jerked her head up and frowned. "What was that?" she whispered.

"Beats me. Turn off the light," Piper whispered.

Rosie tapped the light, and they froze in place.

Straining to listen, Piper startled at a rustle and rasping scrape across the room. "Wind?" Piper whispered.

Rosie gripped Piper's arm and squeezed. "The darkness is scaring us silly. Now we're hearing things. I'm turning on the lights so we can see," she whispered and shuffled toward the door in search of the light switch. She'd taken a couple of steps when a crash in the far corner sent her scurrying back to Piper.

Piper whispered, "Over here."

Rosie grasped the hem of Piper's sweater as she slipped behind a shelf. They peered through the empty shelving into the shadowy room. "Don't turn on the lights and don't move," she whispered.

As their eyes grew accustomed to the dim room, they stared and Piper's pulse raced. She berated herself for sneaking in here against the chief's orders. Rosie squeezed Piper's arm with one hand and clamped her hand over her mouth with the other. She leaned in next to Piper's ear. "Should I text someone? Call?"

Piper whispered, "No." Moving away from Rosie's squeeze, she rubbed her numb arm. As a shadow moved across the murky room, Piper strained to capture a memorable detail. Unfortunately, the storage room had few windows, none on this side.

The shadow appeared to move closer to their hiding spot, but Piper wasn't certain. Rosie clutched Piper's arm and Piper clamped her hand over Rosie's. Surely, the intruder heard the pounding rhythm of her heart. She peered into the darkness and held her breath, her lungs burning. She couldn't exhale and risk giving away their location. When the shadow moved again, Rosie squeezed Piper's arm, digging in her fingernails. From Piper's calculations, the intruder hovered near the figures—inches from their hiding spot. The shelf wobbled, and Piper stiffened.

The prowler mumbled and bumped the shelf in front of their spot. Piper's lungs screamed for air and she strained to avoid inhaling and alerting the creep of their presence. At the moment Piper's lungs collapsed, Rosie's phone rang.

The shadow shot across the storage room. Nativity figures clattered to the floor, Rosie screamed, and Piper whooshed out the breath she'd held.

"Stop!" Rosie yelled, bolting across the storage room.

Piper dropped to the floor, holding her head in her hands, waiting for her heartbeat to settle.

Rosie hollered from the other side of the room. "How did he get out?" She flipped on the overhead lights, and Piper squinted.

"Call Chief Maxwell," Piper said.

Rosie crossed her arms and wrinkled her nose. "No way. Want him to yell at us?" She held her hand out to Piper. "Get up before you get those cute pants dirty."

Piper stood and brushed her hands over the fabric. "How do we know the intruder was a man?"

"We don't, but breaking in a second time is awfully bold, don't you think? What in the world are they after?"

"Let's check these figures again," Piper said, carrying the shepherd to the rickety table in the center of the room. She laid the headless shepherd down and ran her fingers over the surface. "I don't feel anything unusual."

"Knock around on it like they do in mystery movies."

"Seriously, Rosie?" Piper said, rolling her eyes, but she knocked on the figure's surface. "Would we hear a different tone without the head on top?"

"Good point." Rosie leaned her elbows on the other side of the table, watching Piper. She pulled out the notebook and pen. "What shall I write about this little incident?"

"Just the facts, ma'am."

Rosie smiled. "Gotcha, Joe Friday."

"Who?"

"Joe Friday. Dragnet?"

"Never heard of him."

"You never watched old T.V. shows with your parents?"

"Not that one," she said and leaned down, peering closely at the figure. "Shine your light here, please."

Rosie shone the light from her phone on the pitiful shepherd. "See anything?"

"I'm not sure, but look at this spot. Notice anything?" Piper ran her finger over the edge. "Right here, beneath the paint." She scratched gently at the figure and flakes sprinkled over the table.

"What?"

"Come around and see for yourself."

Rosie skipped to Piper's side of the table and hunched over the shepherd.

"Here, I'll hold the light so you can peek." Piper held Rosie's phone above the table.

Rosie eyes widened. "Holy cow. Handwriting?"

"I think so," Piper said, her voice squeaking.

"Can you find another piece to compare?" Rosie held the light close to the edge and gently brushed the wood. "We should stop scratching at this. What if we ruin the finish?"

Piper laughed and lugged one of the Wise Men to the table. "I kind of think they're already ruined."

"What if they're priceless and an expert can restore them?"

"Do you really think so? Why would Fergus donate a priceless nativity set to Cranberry Harbor—even *if* his wife asked him to do it?"

"Maybe he doesn't know the value." Rosie picked at the edge. "What do you see at this broken edge?"

Piper squinted at the splintered edge. "Nothing. This one is plain wood under the paint. What's your opinion?

"Hard to say, but I really think there's a letter underneath the paint on this one."

"What should we do? If they came back again, they must be searching for something important."

"But what?" Rosie asked. "The nativity is pretty and everything, but not valuable."

"The intruder doesn't agree."

"Well, the good news is he's a 'fraidy cat. He ran away the second my phone rang."

"I thought we were in real trouble." Piper patted her heart.

"Oh my goodness," Rosie shrieked. "I almost lost it. What are the odds? The stupid phone rings when we're hiding from a creep!"

"Who called, by the way?"

Rosie picked up her phone from the table and frowned. "You'll never guess."

"One of your brothers?"

"Nope, Chief Maxwell himself."

"What does he want?"

Rosie punched in his number and hit speakerphone. "I don't know, but I'm about to find out."

"I thought you didn't want to get yelled at."

Rosie held up a finger as Chief Maxwell's voice came through the phone.

"Rosie?"

"I missed your call a few moments ago."

"Miss Haydn's phone went to voicemail, too. Let me remind you both to stay out of the investigation. Leave it to my officers."

"Well, actually..."

"Rosie? What's going on?"

"Umm...there might have been another break-in."

"What!" His voice echoed in the storage room. "Why didn't you call me?"

"We might have been hiding in the room during the break-in."

He growled something unintelligible and exploded. "Unbelievable. I'm on the way. Both of you had better be ready with a good explanation. I specifically told you to stay out of our way."

"I know. But good thing we were here, or you'd never know you needed to come back and search for clues." Rosie's chipper voice didn't soothe the angry chief. The call disconnected, and Rosie tapped the phone. "That man needs some sugar or something."

"Look here," Piper said, pointing to the area she'd rubbed clean. "What language is this handwriting?"

Rosie squinted. "Not English." She snapped her fingers. "Hey. I told you I accidentally dusted in Fergus' drawers, right?"

"Yes, and if you remember correctly, I told you snooping was a terrible idea."

"I know. I know. But a few letters in the drawer had old-fashioned, almost identical handwriting." She pointed to the spot. "And those weren't English either."

"What are we going to tell him when he gets here? What about this?" She pointed to the rubbed spot near the shepherd's broken neck.

Rosie shook her head. "No way. We'll share the timeline and what we saw, but we're keeping this delicious discovery to ourselves." She waggled her eyebrows and laughed.

"What if he finds out?"

"If he finds out, we're toast." She giggled. Her joy rang out through the storage room and lightened a smidgeon of Piper's stress.

Chief Maxwell snapped his notebook shut and stood with his hands on his hips, glaring at Piper and Rosie. "The next time I tell you to stay out of my investigation, I expect both of you to listen. You are not law enforcement officers. What would you have done if the intruder had stood his ground? What if he had a weapon?"

Rosie smiled at the officer. "Come on now, Chief. Nothing happened. Surely you're not telling Piper she can't walk into her own storage room, are you?"

He glared, pointing a finger at Rosie. "I give up. You two do whatever you want. Let me know what I'm supposed to tell your families when you get killed or hurt because you refuse to obey orders." He turned, storming from the room, the officers following on his heels.

Rosie whistled. "He's not happy."

"Well, his happiness isn't our problem. It's time to gather supplies for caroling. Can you help, or are you in a hurry?"

"Totally staying to help. Caroling is my favorite event of the year. What's the plan for these guys?" She jerked a thumb toward the row of nativity figures.

"Leave them. I'll ask Don to swing by and check the doors and windows. Do you have time tomorrow? I want to comb over them and try to decipher the hidden writing."

Rosie's eyes sparkled, and she grinned. "Wouldn't miss it for the world."

Piper called Don. "Can you lock the storage room and leave the keys underneath my computer keyboard instead of on the wall hook? If this intruder sneaks in again, they won't find them as easily." She nodded her head. "Good. Thanks, Don." She smiled at Rosie. "Ready to go?"

Rosie linked her arm through Piper's elbow and dragged her down the hallway, humming while she skipped.

Piper's eyes narrowed. "Roosevelt Hale. What are you humming?"

Rosie released Piper's arm and sprinted down the hall, giggling. "You can't stop me, Miss Classical Music."

Piper smiled. Despite her disdain for Rosie's favorite country music, she adored her spirited best friend.

Chapter 4

Still, still, still. One can hear the falling snow.

Saturday Late Afternoon

Volunteers bundled in winter gear spread across the park, setting up tents and tables. Piper directed the crew and Rosie organized the send-off tent. Stacks of music for caroling lined a long table, and she spread the songbooks across the space.

Ruby waved a mittened hand at Rosie. "I brought coffee for the volunteers. You want some?"

Rosie reached for a cup and sipped. "Mmm. I'm thankful it warmed up a bit. No one would have gone caroling in those frigid temperatures."

"You never know. We're a hardy bunch around here. Everyone tries to participate in this one. The Caroling Extravaganza is a great kick-off to our Christmas season," Ruby said.

"It's my favorite too. Thanks for the coffee." Rosie hugged Ruby and returned to organizing the music.

Dominique walked past the tent carrying a tray. "Where is Piper?" she called.

Rosie pointed across the park.

"Stop at our tent for sugar cookies and cocoa later." Dominique lifted the tray and smiled.

"Sure thing, Mrs. Landry. I love your sugar cookies." Rosie licked her lips and rubbed her tummy.

Dominique walked away, chuckling. "Oh, lamb, you're good for my self-esteem."

Robby waved as he passed and jogged to catch up with his wife.

Rosie leaned on the table, watching the activity in the park. Volunteers on ladders hung strings of Christmas lights, set up tents, and arranged chairs and benches around the park. Vendors organized their booths and called to friends. The air buzzed with excitement and Rosie couldn't wait for the Caroling Extravaganza to start. Singing around town and using music to bring cheer to shut-ins and new neighbors filled her heart with joy. She had begged Piper to carol at Fergus' place and assign her to the group. She wanted to see his shock when he opened the door and found neighbors on his porch wishing him a merry Christmas.

By the time the sun set over the park, citizens of Cranberry Harbor filled the space. A small orchestra from the Haydn Music Academy played carols in the gazebo. Neighbors called out to each other. Children ran through the crowd, cookies in hand, their childish squeals adding merriment to the gathering crowd.

At half-past six, the mayor opened the event. "Merry Christmas! Welcome to the annual Cranberry Harbor Caroling Extravaganza."

The crowd burst into applause, and Rosie patted Piper on the back. "You did it, friend. It's amazing."

Piper smiled. "Thank you. But I'm retiring tonight. Not doing this next year."

The mayor raised a hand and said, "Help me count. Three-two-one." As people chanted the countdown, the mayor plugged in the lights, flooding a towering fir tree at the heart of the park with twinkling lights.

When the townspeople cheered. Piper smiled. "I didn't love all the work necessary to pull this off, but these smiles are worth it," she whispered to Rosie.

Rosie nodded, her earrings tinkling as they bumped her scarf. "You're up," she said, pointing to the gazebo.

Piper raced through the crowd and reached the steps as the mayor exclaimed, "A round of applause for the organizer! Piper Haydn saved our annual event from cancelation."

The crowd applauded, and her mother's sharp whistle rang out over the park. Piper blushed. Sarah Haydn blew a kiss from the back of the crowd as Piper reached for the microphone.

"Thank you, everyone. Let's pause and thank God for warming up Wisconsin so we could come out tonight without turning into icicles."

Chuckles rippled through the park, and Piper stepped aside for Pastor James to open the event in prayer.

"And we pray for safety as we travel through town spreading love and cheer to neighbors who aren't well enough to join us. Amen."

Piper reclaimed the microphone and explained the plan for the evening.

"Your group captain will collect addresses and songbooks from the tent at the entrance. When you've finished caroling, return to the park for cocoa and cookies. Now, go spread Christmas cheer." She wrapped her scarf around her rosy cheeks, watching the crowd disperse to their vehicles. She breathed a sigh of relief. With the tree lighting ceremony over, and carolers on their way to spread cheer, she'd accomplished a chunk of her December to-do list. Only a couple of concerts and a Christkindlmarket to go. Then she could unwind and enjoy her Christmas season.

She headed to the sendoff tent to collect Rosie and their caroling group. Her heart flooded with thankfulness at the smooth start of the event. She glanced around the park and frowned. A woman stood next to a blue cargo van across the street, staring at the crowd. Piper shivered, turning away from the coatless woman. She walked towards the tent, but when she looked back, the woman and van had vanished. She exhaled. "Now you're imagining things, Piper Haydn."

"What?" Rosie said.

"Nothing. Everyone ready?"

Rosie clapped her hands. "Yes, let's go. I have Christmas carols bubbling in my soul."

"Everything bubbles in your soul, Miss Rosie," Robby said.

Piper laughed. "You figured her out, Robby."

He smiled, his kind brown eyes twinkling. "Let me find my wife and we can be on our way."

Piper reached for the address list Rosie held. "I'm pretty excited. This has been my favorite part of the Christmas season since I was a little girl."

"I'm glad you rescued it from oblivion then, my friend." Rosie collected their stack of songbooks as Robby and Dominique entered the tent.

"Four in our group?" Dominique asked, glancing around the emptying park.

"Piper decided if we split into smaller groups, we can sing our carols and get back here to gobble cocoa and cookies sooner."

Dominique's rich laugh rang out. "Good thinking."

The group followed Rosie to her car and piled inside. "First stop, Mrs. Harris."

"Oh, she's so sweet. Why is she unable to come tonight?" Dominique asked.

Piper turned in the passenger seat. "She slipped on ice last week and twisted her ankle."

Dominique scowled. "One thing I'll say about moving up here from Louisiana. I hate ice."

Robby chuckled. "And what else do you hate, darlin'?"

Dominique gasped. "What are you talking about, fine sir?"

He held up his fingers, counting down. "Bland food, boring music at church."

"Robby," she shrieked and swatted her husband's arm. Piper and Rosie laughed in the front seat.

"Do tell, Mr. Robby. What else?"

"You hush now," Dominique said.

Robby pretended to zip his lips, but his eyes sparkled. "I'll tell you later," he said in a loud stage whisper as he leaned up towards Rosie's ear.

A car pulled alongside them, and Rosie leaned out. "Hey. What's up?"

Sarah Haydn rolled down her window. "I forgot to invite everyone over after church tomorrow for pasta. You too, Dominique and Robby."

"I never miss an opportunity to eat your pasta, Mrs. Haydn." Rosie looked at her passengers. "Dominique?"

"Not this time. We have plans for tomorrow, but thank you for the invitation."

"We'll miss you. See you later, girls," Sarah Haydn said, waving as Piper's dad drove away.

"Where did you send your parents?" Rosie asked.

"To the assisted living. I figured Mom would have more fun if she stayed warm."

"Your mother is a wise woman," Dominique said.

"I'll keep you warm, honey." Robby reached to hug his wife.

Dominique shooed him away. "Not in front of the children."

Robby's chuckle filled the car, and Rosie grinned at Piper.

"Mrs. Harris lives out near Fergus. You're not stopping at his place, are you?" Dominique asked.

Piper and Rosie looked at each other. Piper cleared her throat. "Well, actually, we are Mrs. Landry, but you can blame Rosie. She said Fergus needs a little cheer whether or not he wants it."

"Oh brother," Dominique said. "I should have stayed at the park. Fergus annoys me. No reason for a man to carry so much anger in his heart. But he doesn't just hold anger. He slings his feelings all over town."

"Now, honey. Jesus loves Mr. Fergus as much as he loves us," Robby said, patting Dominique's arm.

"Don't you 'now honey' me about him. I've tried. Honest I've tried. You know, last time he came into Sweetberry's, he ate three cinnamon rolls, drank two cups of coffee and left without paying his bill because he said the rolls seemed a little stale. He has plenty of money to pay for those cinnamon rolls. Stale my eye." She harrumphed and crossed her arms.

"I've tried too, but he's a tough one. He doesn't like any of the Haydns."

"How are you getting on working for him, Miss Rosie?" Robby asked.

Rosie smiled. "I enjoy working at his place, but I don't really see him. He disappears, but he's nice enough when he comes out." She giggled. "Well, he's nice for Fergus."

Robby chuckled. "You know, he talks to me when I bump into him in town—usually at the hardware store. I imagine he's lonely since his wife died."

"I don't remember her," Piper said. "Do you?"

"No, she was bedridden before we moved to town. No one knows what ailed her, but rumors say she was ill for a long while."

"He could treat people right." Dominique huffed. "But I promise I'll behave when we're at his house. I won't even ask him to pay for his cinnamon rolls."

"There's my girl," Robby said.

"You heard what happened to the nativity set?" Piper asked.

Dominique nodded.

"Rosie and I can't figure out why anyone would want to damage it."

"Lazy people with nothing to do, I suppose," Dominique said. "Looks like Mrs. Harris is expecting us."

The porch light shone into the yard, and a small white-haired woman waited at the door.

"I love her," Rosie said.

They piled out of the car singing a lively verse of "Joy to the World" as they walked to her door. Their breath froze as they sang, swirling around their heads in wispy puffs.

Rosie licked a peppermint stick as they walked to the car. "Mrs. Harris always gave me candy at church." She smiled. "I do adore a candy cane or two at Christmas."

"They're extra good in a mug of hot chocolate," Dominque said from the backseat.

Rosie grimaced. "Chocolate. Blech."

"You're a mystery, Miss Rosie," Dominique said. "Chocolate is one of the greatest joys of life."

"As long as my chocolate hate is the sole mystery around here."

"Amen, Miss Rosie," Robby said.

Rosie gripped the steering wheel. "Next stop Fergus. You ready? Brace yourselves."

"I have confidence Fergus will thank us for spreading Christmas cheer," Piper proclaimed.

Rosie raised an eyebrow. "Umm.... Piper? This is Fergus you're talking about."

Piper leaned her head against the headrest, closing her eyes.

"Whoa," Rosie shrieked, and the car rocked as a blue blur sped past. Rosie tapped the brakes and pulled to the side of the road. "What in the world?"

"Looked like a van to me," Robby said.

"A blue van. Not a family van, but the cargo type," Dominique said. "Speeding on winter roads? What's the matter with people?"

"Way too fast for the snow and ice," Robby said.

"Everyone alright?" Rosie asked.

"I'm fine. Could it be the same van I noticed at the park tonight? Too bad I closed my eyes. I missed it."

"What van? You didn't say anything about a van at the park. What was that you just said about mysteries?" Rosie asked.

Piper groaned. "Boring. I want a boring life. No excitement. No mysteries."

"Hang in there, baby." Dominique leaned up and patted her shoulder.

Piper rested her hand over Dominique's. "Thank you."

Rosie pulled onto the road and pointed. "Onward and upward and all that jazz. To Fergus' house we go."

"Lord, help us all," Robby whispered in the backseat.

CHAPTER 5

Saturday Evening

Rosie turned into Fergus' property and inched down the driveway. She parked on the side of his garage and pasted on a perky smile. "Here we are. Everyone ready?"

"Ready as we'll ever be," Piper said, picking up her songbook.

The group huddled together and walked to Fergus' massive front door.

"Doesn't look like he's home. No lights," Robby whispered.

"He's home. He hardly ever leaves," Rosie whispered back.

Dominique leaned between them and whispered, "Why are we whispering?"

Piper laughed, but her hand shook, and a chill skittered up her spine.

Stepping onto the porch, Rosie turned. "Everyone, be calm. Smile. Sing. And get out of here."

Piper leaned forward and tapped the doorbell. A deep chime rang inside the house. She peered through the sidelight windows. "Robby's right, he's not home. Did anyone notice Fergus at the park?"

"Fergus? Caroling? I think you've lost your mind, Miss Piper," Dominique said.

Rosie frowned. Reaching around Piper, she stabbed the doorbell three times. "Come on, Fergus. Open up. We're freezing out here."

Robby stepped into the yard and tipped his head back. He frowned. "No lights up there."

"I'll run around back and take a peek. Wait here," Rosie said. She turned and tromped through the snow, disappearing around the corner of the house.

Piper rubbed her arms and shivered. "Should she go alone?"

"I'll go," Robby said, trudging through the snow.

Piper inched closer to Dominique. "The two of us standing out here alone doesn't make me feel any better."

Dominique squeezed Piper's hand. "Everything's fine. We are spooking ourselves because Fergus isn't our favorite neighbor."

"I suppose. I'll admit I'm nervous about what he'll say when he discovers me on his porch. With the nativity set destroyed, I'm expecting a withering tirade."

"Nah. I suspect Fergus is all bark and no bite."

"I'm not so sure," Piper said. "But I'll find a way to make things right. I don't want him having more excuses to hold a grudge against my family."

Rosie popped around the corner. "No lights on back there and I couldn't see through the kitchen windows."

"Ring the bell once more," Robby suggested, stepping onto the porch.

Dominique reached out to press the bell and yanked her hand to her side. "Umm..." She pointed. "The door." She tapped the wood with one finger, and the door creaked open.

"Not creepy at all," Rosie said, stepping closer to Piper.

"What should we do?" Piper asked Robby.

He moved around the huddled women and peered in the open door. "Mr. Standerwick?"

"Nothing," Rosie whispered.

Robby cupped his hands around his mouth. "Mr. Standerwick. Robby Landry here. Are you home?"

Piper pulled her arm out of Rosie's grip. "Ouch. You're cutting off my circulation. Not so tight."

"Sorry," Rosie said. "I'm scared."

"No need for fright, Miss Rosie," Robby said. "He's most likely resting. You ladies stay behind me. Does he have trouble hearing, Rosie?"

"I haven't noticed, but like I said, he's not around much when I'm here."

Taking a small step into the entryway, Robby called again. "Mr. Standerwick. Fergus. We're here to sing Christmas carols for you. You home?"

The ticking grandfather clock echoed in the silent hall.

Rosie squealed. "I don't like this at all."

"Where's his room?" Robby asked.

"His bedroom is the last door off the hallway upstairs, but his den is the last room on this wing. What are we going to do?"

"I'm fixin' to look for him. He's probably fast asleep."

"And we're going to wake him up and get yelled at for roaming his house without his permission," Piper said.

"Do you ladies want to wait for me or go together?" Robby asked.

"Stay together," the women said in unison.

"My dear Mr. Landry," Dominique said. "Don't you think we should call the police?"

Piper frowned. "And have Chief Maxwell remind us to stay out of it?"

Dominique turned, a question in her eyes, but spoke to Robby. "Well?"

"No, ma'am. Let me peek around. If we see anything suspicious, we'll call."

"Alright," Dominique said. "Why did I marry the brave one?"

Rosie giggled. "I'm thankful he's brave."

"Me too, honey," Dominique said. "But he worries me now and then."

Robby tiptoed up the staircase, the women tip toed behind him, holding their breath.

Goosebumps rose on Piper's arms and a chill raced up her spine, but she followed her friends. Her heart hammered in her throat and she held onto Rosie, wishing they hadn't come. "Whose bright idea was this, anyway?" she whispered.

Rosie nudged her. "Shh."

When they reached the landing, Robby asked, "Which way?"

Rosie pointed. They walked past several closed doors, and Piper's pulse raced.

"Here's his room," Rosie said. "I've never gone inside."

Robby knocked on the door. "Mr. Standerwick. It's Robby Landry. Are you home? Mr. Standerwick?"

Silence.

Dominique's brown eyes widened, and she frowned. "Come on, Robby. He's not home. Let's get out of here."

Robby knocked again and jiggled the handle. The door swung open into a dim room.

Rosie sucked in a breath. "If he's sleeping and we wake him, you know he'll have us arrested for trespassing."

Robby tiptoed into the room and whispered, "Mr. Standerwick. Fergus."

Dominique flipped the light switch and Rosie screamed.

"Empty," Robby said.

Rosie held her hand over her heart, gasping for breath. "Dominique, when you turned the light on, I had a heart attack."

Dominique chuckled, and her eyes sparkled. "I didn't mean to frighten you two, but the look on your faces was a sight to behold."

Piper held her stomach. "I've had enough adrenaline for one day. Let's get out of here."

"We didn't check the den. I believe we better investigate before we leave," Robby said, leading the way.

Piper grabbed Rosie's arm as they walked down the staircase.

"Where do you think he is?" Piper asked. "I know I didn't see Fergus at the park."

"Didn't you say his sister-in-law is visiting? Maybe they went out of town for dinner?" Dominique suggested.

Rosie frowned. "Like a date?"

"No, but people *do* go out for dinner without going on a date," Dominque said.

Piper nudged Rosie in the ribs.

"You and the chief definitely went on a date," Rosie said.

Piper ignored Rosie's tease and hurried after Robby.

"Which way, Miss Rosie?" he asked.

Rosie took the lead, walking across the large entryway and hurrying through two large rooms and another hall. "There," she said, pointing to a heavy wooden door. She hid behind Dominique and Piper. "I'm not going in, though."

Robby turned to the women. "Be calm. I'm going to flip the lights on. No screaming." His smile lessened the severity of the scolding.

Robby reached for the brass doorknob, and Piper held her breath. Rosie squeezed Piper's hand, and they pressed closer to Dominique. The heavy door scraped across the floor, and they clustered together, waiting for the lights.

"I can't find the switch," Robby whispered.

Rosie stepped inside the open door. "Oops. The switch is half-way down the bookshelf next to a picture frame."

Piper gripped Rosie's hand and held her breath.

Robby muttered as a crash rang out. "Knocked something over, I think."

The overhead light illuminated the den, and Piper gasped. She pointed to Fergus slumped on a green leather Chesterfield sofa. The broken Mary and Baby Jesus figures lay smashed at his feet.

"Fergus!" Rosie yelled, running to the couch.

"Don't touch him," Robby cautioned.

Dominique gasped. "Oh, no."

"Call the police. Quick," Robby ordered.

Piper held her phone and dialed with shaky fingers.

"9-1-1. What's the address of the emergency?"

"We are at Fergus Standerwick's. He's not conscious," Piper said, her voice cracking.

"Address?"

Piper's hand shook. "What's his address, Rosie?"

"I don't know."

"We don't know," she yelled. Tears pooled in her eyes and her heart pounded. "Please hurry."

"Tell me exactly what happened."

"We came to sing Christmas carols and found him on the sofa."

"Are you with the patient now?"

"Yes, we're here. All of us are here."

"How old is he?"

Piper bit her lip. "How old?"

"How old is the patient?"

"I don't know." She paced back and forth. "I don't know. Oh, hurry."

"Is he awake?"

"No," Piper shouted. "He's slumped over."

"Is he breathing?"

"She wants to know if he's breathing," Piper said, hitting the speakerphone, allowing Robby to hear the dispatcher.

"Paramedics are on the way. Let's check his breathing. When I say go, watch and tell me if his chest rises."

Robby stepped to the sofa and leaned over Fergus. He nodded.

"He's breathing," Piper yelled.

"Is he breathing at a normal rate?"

Robby shook his head.

"No. How close are they?" Piper tugged at the scarf around her neck and closed her eyes as spots floated across her vision.

"Stay on the line until the paramedics are with you. I'll tell you what to do. Listen carefully." The calm voice filled the room. "Lay him flat on the floor, nothing under his head. Can you do that?"

"Yes," Piper shouted and hurried to the sofa as Robby and Dominique slid Fergus to the ground.

Rosie collected pillows from a chair near the window to prop at his side.

"Tilt his head back. Watch closely. Is he breathing?"

Piper squeezed the base of her neck as Robby leaned over Fergus. When Robby nodded, Piper said, "Yes. Yes, he's breathing." She fanned her face as heat rose, and her heart hammered.

"I'll stay on the line. Tell me when the paramedics are with him."

Dominique hovered near Robby with her hands clasped. "Dear Father, please help. Oh God, please help us."

Her repeated prayer soothed Piper's racing mind. *Yes, Father. Please help.* She gasped. "I hear sirens," she yelled.

"Don't leave him until the paramedics are at his side."

"Okay, but tell them to hurry."

"They're on the way, ma'am."

Red and blue lights swirled through the windows and reflected on the wall. Piper blew out a breath.

"Cranberry Harbor Fire Department," a voice shouted.

Rosie ran to the hall. "In here."

As paramedics rushed down the hall, the four friends stepped away from Fergus and huddled in a circle, praying quietly until a tap on Piper's shoulder interrupted their prayer.

Chief Maxwell stood behind her, an eyebrow raised. "Miss Haydn? What's going on?"

Rosie and Piper talked at once, shouting out bits of their discovery.

"The light wasn't on..."

"Slumped on the sofa..."

"Someone smashed the baby Jesus..."

Chief Maxwell held up his hand. "One at a time, please."

Dominique stepped forward. "Sir, we came to sing carols tonight for Fergus, but he didn't answer the door. Rosie works here and went around back to check for lights. By the time she returned, we discovered the open door."

"Fergus doesn't trust anyone. He always locks his doors," Rosie said.

"You entered?" Chief Maxwell asked.

Piper nodded. "Yes, but we called his name several times first."

"No answer," Rosie said.

"And then?"

"We came in to make sure Fergus was safe."

The chief scratched his forehead and tapped the pen on his notepad. "How did you know to come straight here?" He frowned.

"We didn't. We went upstairs to his room first, but he wasn't there," Piper said.

"Obviously." Rosie giggled nervously and clapped her hand over her mouth.

Piper nudged Rosie, stepping in front of her to allow her time to regain her composure. "Rosie said he spends a lot of time in the den and suggested we search here next. The lights were off and when Robby found the switch, we found..." She motioned to the couch.

Chief Maxwell walked away and joined the paramedics.

"Why do I get the feeling we're in trouble?" Piper asked Dominique.

"Hold on, lamb. God knows the truth."

Rosie leaned in and whispered, "The nativity scene *did* have something to do with this."

"Yeah. But...but what?" Piper stammered. She rubbed her arms as her stomach clenched. Paramedics loaded Fergus on the stretcher.

One buckled the straps across his legs, and another eased an oxygen mask over Fergus' pale face.

"As much as I don't like him, I hate to see this. I don't want him hurt." Piper wiped a tear from the corner of her eye.

Dominique enveloped Piper with strong, brown arms and squeezed. "We know you didn't want Fergus hurt. Put it out of your mind, sugar."

"How do we know someone hurt him?" Rosie asked. "Maybe he had a heart attack while hacking up the nativity figures."

Piper's eyes narrowed, and she frowned at the pile of splintered wood near the sofa. Baby Jesus' face stared up from the debris. "Interesting hypothesis, Roosevelt."

"No hypothesizing. I mean it. I've warned you two to stay out of this." Chief Maxwell pointed at Piper. "Don't force me to take further action to keep you two out of my investigation. Do you understand?"

Piper and Rosie nodded.

"Something tells me neither one of you intends to obey my directions, but I assure you I will keep my promise next time. Stay out of it." He strode down the hall behind the paramedics, the ambulance filling the room with swirling red lights.

Rosie mimicked the chief's stern look.

Piper jabbed her with an elbow. "He's doing his job." She glanced past Rosie to an open door. "Was the sliding glass door open the entire time we were here?"

Rosie looked toward the door and frowned. "Robby? Dominique? Did you notice?"

Robby rubbed his jaw and stared at the door. "I can't say, Miss Rosie. I went straight to Fergus."

Piper watched the busy room. Officers wrote in their notebooks. One measured the distance from the destroyed figures to the couch, while another snapped photos. She whispered in Rosie's ear, "Look around and take note. I'll do the same. We'll debrief at my place later."

Rosie nodded and turned in the opposite direction, scanning the room.

Piper turned in a circle, searching for clues. Her eyes narrowed at the dainty china teacup and saucer on the side table next to Fergus' end of the sofa. She tapped Rosie's arm and pointed. "Does Fergus drink tea?"

"I haven't noticed," Rosie frowned. "But what a dainty cup for a curmudgeon. Think someone else was here before us?"

Piper craned her neck. "Do you see another teacup anywhere in here?"

Rosie scanned the room. "Nope."

Piper cleared her throat, and an officer looked her way. "Yes?"

Heat rose in her cheeks. Was she disobeying the police chief? Maybe, but she had to say something. She pointed to the end table. "Excuse me for interrupting. Did you notice the teacup on the end table?"

The officer stared. "We have this under control, Miss Haydn. Step out of the room and wait for an officer, please."

"I shouldn't have said anything," Piper said when they slipped into the hallway.

"You had to mention what you noticed, Piper. At least the chief didn't hear you meddling."

"Meddling in what?" a gruff voice called from the front door.

"Now you've done it," Rosie said.

Piper stammered, "I...um...I...I pointed out a teacup on the side table."

He glared in their direction. "Miss Haydn." His voice carried a warning.

"I know. Stay out of your investigation."

"Wait here. Someone will speak with you shortly." He hurried past them and slammed the door.

After giving their statements to an officer, Chief Maxwell dismissed the group. The Caroling Extravaganza had ended, but Piper wanted to swing by the park to check on the clean-up crew's progress.

"I didn't get to share my thank you speech and invite everyone to the *Messiah* performance or the Christkindlmarket," Piper whined.

Dominique hushed Piper from the backseat. "We'll help you get the word out. All the business owners on Main Street have concert fliers to pass out and the whole town knows about the Christkindlmarket. Everything's gonna work out the way it's supposed to."

"Yeah," Rosie said. "The market is going to be amazing. We have bigger things to deal with. Like who did this to Fergus and why did someone destroy the nativity set?"

"You heard Chief Maxwell, girls. I know you couldn't help yourselves the last two times things went wrong, but this matter isn't for you ladies to get tangled up in."

"You're right, as usual, Robby, but it's hard. Especially when the academy's reputation is at stake—again," Piper said.

"You can always give it to God and let him handle it," he suggested.

His gentle voice almost convinced Piper to release her anxiety. "Thank you, Mr. Landry."

"We're praying for you. But your safety matters, too."

Rosie eased her car next to the curb at the park. "All clean. I guess we can go home and put this weird evening behind us. Did anyone say how we can check on Fergus?"

"I doubt they'll tell us, but the Cranberry Harbor grapevine might know by morning," Piper said.

"Or we can read about it in the stupid Cranberry Harbor Tattler," Rosie said.

Dominique and Robby climbed out of the backseat. "Thanks for the ride, girls. I'm truly praying for you," Robby said, leaning into Rosie's open window.

"Call me when you get home, please," Dominique said. "I want to know you're safe and snug at home."

"Yes, ma'am." Rosie saluted and rolled up her window. She shivered and cranked the knob on the heater. "So, what are we doing?"

Piper smiled and twisted her fingers in her lap. "We're going to my place and comparing notes."

Rosie pumped her fist in the air. "Yes!" Her earrings jingled and her eyes sparkled. "I have a lot of buzzing in my brain. I can't wait to work on all these puzzle pieces."

Rosie rummaged through Piper's dresser drawers. "What in the world, Piper? You have boring pajamas." Rosie held up a green t-shirt with the slogan, "I just want to bake something and watch Christmas movies," and a pair of red sweatpants. "Well, this is the most festive thing I found. Where's your cozy sock bin?" She spun around and gasped, staggering backward in mock horror. "You mean to tell me you don't wear big fluffy socks when you live in this drafty old house? What are you, a psychopath?"

Piper rolled her eyes. "Cozy socks annoy my feet. Hurry! Let's compare notes and get to bed. Morning comes early."

Rosie slipped into Piper's pajamas and twisted her curls into a ponytail. "All right, Jessica Fletcher, Murder She Wrote, and all that jazz. Let's solve a mystery."

The girls settled in the turret, arranging a large quilt over their legs. Rosie tucked the blanket around her cold feet and opened the notebook. "It's been quite the day. What to write?"

Piper stared out the window, gathering her thoughts. "For starters...the papers you found in his drawers and the mysterious writing underneath the shepherd."

"Got it," Rosie said. "What else?"

"Fergus," Piper said. "The blue van."

Rosie chewed on the end of the pen and stared at Piper. "The open sliding glass door, the cup of tea." Rosie closed her eyes. "Was the teacup empty or full?"

"I didn't get close enough to check." She rubbed the back of her neck. "Two things we need to solve. What's hiding under the paint and what's up with the blue van?"

"Think the van has anything to do with Fergus?"

"They were speeding down the road near his house. And seems a strange coincidence if it's the same van I saw at the park, doesn't it?"

"Maybe they came to check out the commotion?" Rosie dropped the notebook and stretched. "My brain hurts."

"Mine too. I need to practice my pieces before bed. Do you mind?"

"Of course not, my virtuoso friend. Lull me to sleep. I'm sleeping right here, if you don't object." She flopped onto the couch and closed her eyes.

The smooth keys under Piper's fingers calmed her scattered brain. She ran through a chorus from The *Messiah* "Comfort Ye My People". Her strong fingers pounded out the octaves and running notes. Piper finished the piece, marveling at Handel's brilliance. Teaching a choir to sing his music and playing the piece took plenty of practice. She couldn't imagine the brain power necessary to compose the oratorio. She ran through her Hanon finger exercises with her eyes closed until she yawned. Time to put her tired self to bed and leave this strange day behind.

She closed the piano lid and tiptoed to the doorway, turning off the lights. Blowing a kiss to her childhood best friend, she whispered, "Sweet dreams." Questions about the clues and distress over Fergus jabbed holes in her peace as she climbed the stairs. The loose step creaked under her foot, and Piper balanced on the edge before finishing the climb.

"See," Rosie called from the turret. "I told you. Perfect security system." Her giggle floated up the stairway.

Piper laughed. "Good night, goofball."

"Same to you, goober."

CHAPTER 6

The night is peaceful all around you. Close your eyes, let sleep surround you.

Sunday Morning

Piper blinked as sunlight flooded her room. She rolled over to check the time and bumped into Rosie standing at the edge of her bed. "What are you doing?" she croaked, her voice heavy with exhaustion.

"So rise and shine and give God the glory glory. Rise and shine..." Rosie sang the old Sunday School song at the top of her lungs—waving her arms and dancing around the room.

"My word. Stop. I'll get up." Piper swung her legs over the side of the bed. "Why did you open my shades?" She rubbed her eyes.

"We have an investigation to discuss. I couldn't sleep. I had clues ricocheting through my dreams all night. We need to talk."

Piper held up a hand. "Not before coffee."

Rosie picked up a paper cup from the bedside table and handed it to Piper.

"You've been to Ruby's already?"

Rosie smiled. "I told you I couldn't sleep. I ordered a gingerbread latte for you. Flavor of the day."

Piper took a sip of the spicy drink. "Mmm. Exquisite. Did you get one for yourself?"

Rosie nodded and held up another cup. "Dirty chai for me."

Piper scooted over and patted her bed. "Hop in and talk."

Rosie climbed into the four-poster bed and wiggled her toes under the cover. "Mmm. It's toasty in here."

"Spill it. Not the coffee." She grinned at Rosie.

"I'm not Amelia Bedelia, you know. I wouldn't literally obey you." She sipped the latte and leaned her head on the pile of pillows. "What did I hear you playing last night, by the way? I could listen to you all day."

"Comfort Ye My People."

"From the *Messiah*?" Rosie opened an eye and peeked at Piper.

"Yep. The only music I'm playing right now." She stretched her fingers. "I need to practice this afternoon."

"You ever tire of practicing?"

"You ever tire of painting?"

"Never."

"Same." Piper smiled. "Okay, coffee's working." She checked the clock. "Hurry though. I need to get dressed."

"We should review the security recordings Lisa downloaded. See if anyone else shows up."

"How about after lunch this afternoon? Are you free?"

"Absolutely." She smoothed the quilt over her and snuggled into the cozy bed. "I'm curious to see what's under the paint on the shepherd. I pictured it in my mind over and over. What if we remove the varnish on top? Can we decipher the handwriting? But considering the Fergus situation, how closely do you think the police will investigate this? Should we examine the shepherd before we review the recordings?"

Piper sat up. "Yes. But if I don't get moving right now, I'll never get to church on time." She dug through her closet and chose a white blouse and a red pencil skirt.

Rosie groaned and jumped out of bed. "Pencil skirt again? You need bell bottoms or something. Anything." She reached into the closet and handed Piper a pair of green ballet flats. "At least wear these and this," she said, holding out a Christmas print scarf.

Piper took the scarf and slid her feet into the shoes. "Perfect thanks. Are you changing?"

"Stop by my place on the way, and I'll run in. We'll make it to church on time if we leave in ten minutes."

"Sure, Rosie. I don't need to do my hair or slap on makeup."

Rosie kissed Piper's cheek and giggled. "You're gorgeous the way you are, and Chief Maxwell agrees."

"Rosie," Piper warned.

"Hey, I quit calling him hunky at your request, m'lady. But I'll never stop calling you gorgeous. How about I run home and change and swing back for you?"

"Thanks," Piper said, as she tied the scarf around her neck. "I hope we hear an update on Fergus this morning."

Rosie's eyes widened. "Oh, Piper. I hope he didn't die."

Piper nodded and whispered a prayer, "Father, please help."

Worship music played over the speakers in the church foyer. "Aargh. We're late," Rosie said, slipping off her Kelly-green wool coat trimmed in fluffy feathers. She spun around, her red and green plaid skirt floating around her legs in a perfect circle.

"What a beautiful skirt."

Rosie bowed. "Thank you. This Cranberry Closet special is a wrap-around vintage wool Pendleton. You like?"

"I'd wear it."

Rosie's jaw dropped. "Say it isn't so. Miss Haydn would wear something from the thrift store?" She gathered her Bible from the top of the coat rack. "We better hurry or we'll be late and our mothers will holler at us."

They slipped into the pew next to Sarah Haydn moments before the worship leader said, "Let's stand and greet one another."

Milling around in the hall after the service, Piper chatted with friends. The Caroling Extravaganza and Fergus dominated the conversations. Piper scanned the crowd for Will Maxwell, hoping for an update on Fergus. Her stomach tightened when she noticed him surrounded by church leadership.

Rosie stepped up behind her. "Doesn't look good, does it?"

"No. Looks like something went wrong."

"Did you read the Tattler this morning?"

"No. Is it about Fergus?"

Rosie held out her phone.

Town Elder hospitalized after a run-in with a member of the "esteemed" Haydn family.

Fergus Standerwick remains hospitalized this morning after a run-in with Piper Haydn and her entourage. Details remain sketchy, but sources report that Fergus was found unresponsive in his home at some point in the evening. We know Fergus let the group inside, presumably to allow them to sing Christmas carols. Investigators are still determining what transpired between the moment he opened the door and the moment the authorities discovered Mr. Standerwick unresponsive. We send our prayers to Fergus' loved ones, including his oldest son Everett who arrived in Cranberry Harbor this week to celebrate Christmas with his father.

The question on everyone's mind—what did Piper Haydn do to Fergus and what does she have against this elder pillar of our community? Stay tuned for details. We'll update as news crosses our desk.

The Cranberry Harbor Tattler

"Come on. How do they know these details? How do they know who was there?"

"They got one thing wrong. Fergus didn't let us in."

Piper's eyes widened, and she pointed at the screen. "His son? His son is in town? Did you see a son last night?"

Rosie frowned. "Hey, you're right. Where was he?"

Piper clenched her jaw and stared at the knot of people surrounding the chief. "I want answers." She marched down the hall and waited until Chief Maxwell noticed her. She stared, waiting for him to step away from the cluster of people.

He cleared his throat. "Excuse me, gentlemen." He walked over to Piper and nodded. "Yes? You need something?"

Rosie leaned forward and said, "Yeah. Answers."

"I'm unable to share anything with you at this time, ladies. You know how this works."

"Have you seen the blog this morning?" Piper's eyes narrowed. "How am I to blame for this? Who's writing this Tattler? How are they privy to details?"

"How is Fergus?" Rosie asked.

The chief held up a hand. "You know I'm not at liberty to say."

Piper rested her hands on her hips. "If you don't tell us, I'll call Betty. She cleans patient rooms at night and knows everything."

"Betty can't tell you either." He pinched the bridge of his nose and his voice lowered to a whisper. "He's not well. I can't tell you anything else."

"Did you confiscate the teacup from the side table?" Rosie asked.

"You've been watching too many crime shows," he said.

"Come on. What does it hurt to check the contents of the cup?"

"Time. Money. But if it makes you happy, yes. We took the cup." He turned to Piper. "Miss Haydn, we'd like to collect the other nativity figures tomorrow. I'll send an officer to the academy during business hours." He walked away, but stopped. "Don't make me remind you what I said about this investigation." He disappeared down the hall.

"Hey," Rosie said. "We better examine the nativity scene this afternoon. Right after we feast on your mother's pasta."

Rosie reached into the cupboard and chose a mug for her latte. "What's my destination this time?" She read the caption on the mug and smiled. "Paris. When did you get this one, Mrs. Haydn?"

Sarah hustled past Rosie carrying a bowl of pasta. "Let me see?"

Rosie held the pottery mug up high and Sarah glanced back as she set the food on the dining room table.

"I bought it at a charming little shop on the trip we took before Chase was born."

Rosie held the mug under Sarah's fancy machine and waited for the coffee to brew.

Piper handed Rosie a carton of cream and the frothing machine. "Make me one?"

"Of course."

"Me too," Chase called as he breezed past Rosie and kissed Sarah on the cheek.

"Make your own, Chase," Rosie said. "I'm taking care of your sister's latte and then I'm claiming my seat at the table and stealing your baby nephew."

"Whatever," Chase said, and reached into the salad bowl, picking out croutons.

"Chase Haydn," Sarah called from the doorway. "Get your hands out of the dinner."

He smiled and licked his fingers. "What can I carry to the table, Mom?"

Sarah pointed to the steaming bowls of pasta on the counter. "And grab serving spoons."

The back door opened, and Braden and his family filled the kitchen. The energy of the little boys boosted the joyful atmosphere. After a round of hugs, Sarah directed everyone to the table.

Jack Haydn waited as his family filled in the seats. He reached out to hold Sarah's hand, and the family gathered to pray.

"Amen," Asher said, when Jack finished and everyone laughed at the small boy.

"Piper," her father said. "What's going on at the academy?"

"My business or the investigation?"

He glanced over his glasses with a tight smile. "Investigation."

"According to Chief Maxwell, he's arranging for an officer to come tomorrow and collect the remaining figures. Have you heard any news about Fergus' condition?"

"No, but I'm not surprised. I'll see what I can find out in the morning. It's all so very odd. I don't understand what the nativity set has to do with Fergus."

"Did you really see him slumped over?" Chase asked.

"Chase," Jack Haydn warned. "The children."

The baby smacked his spoon on the tray and squealed. Sarah stood and kissed him on the forehead. "Pass the food before I'm forced to rewarm your dinner."

Braden cleared his throat. "How do we discover who's behind this Tattler?"

Emily frowned. "I'm suspicious. How do they know these details?"

"Exactly," Rosie said, heaping her plate with pasta and ladling red marinara sauce over the top. "Someone needs a knuckle sandwich."

Landon's eyes widened, and he stared at Rosie. She winked, and they both giggled. "Oops, Mr. Landon. Knuckle sandwiches are too violent for a nice young man like yourself."

"You're funny, Miss Rosie," he said.

She blew him a kiss and leaned toward Asher, blowing another.

"No more heavy discussion at the table." Jack said. "What are your Christmas plans, Roosevelt?"

Rosie's eyes sparkled. "Well, as you know, Christkindlmarket is coming up. I'm adding final details to custom orders for several vendors. My art students at the academy are working on their pieces to display at the market. I'm helping your daughter with a million details and when we put the finishing touches on all these activities, my siblings and I are hightailing it out of here. Mom rented a cabin up north where we'll spend four days stuffing our faces with too many treats, staying up too late playing games, and watching too many Christmas movies."

Sarah smiled. "What a lovely holiday. Enjoy." She picked up a bowl of pasta and passed it to her husband. "Piper, is the choir ready for their big performance?"

"As ready as we'll ever be. They're doing well, but I need to question my sanity next time I sign up to lead a market and produce a concert on top of my daily duties."

"Emily, are you spending Christmas Eve with your family?" Piper asked.

Emily wiped a smear of applesauce from the baby's cheek. "Yes, and then here for Christmas day."

Rosie nudged Piper and whispered, "We need to..." She nodded her head toward the door.

Sarah stood and gathered the dirty dishes. "Piper, if you and Rosie need to leave, go ahead. I know you have lots on your plate right now."

"Thank you for dinner, Mrs. Haydn. If you ever need a taste tester for your pasta, you know who to call," Rosie said.

Sarah kissed Piper's cheek and patted her back. "Love you, sweetheart. Stay safe."

"I'd like you to listen to Chief Maxwell, Piper Grace," Jack said from the head of the table. "Stay out of his way."

"We aren't in his way," Piper said, stepping away from the table to escape her father's warning.

"Piper."

She ran to his chair and squeezed her father's shoulders. "I love you, Dad." She blew a kiss to her nephews and followed Rosie to the car.

"Phew. Close call," Rosie said, laughing. "Your dad worries about you."

"Everyone worries about me. Onward, my friend. We have clues to analyze."

Pulling onto the street, Rosie fiddled with the radio dial. "You know what I wish?"

"Hmm?"

"I wish my favorite band from Milwaukee would record a Christmas album. But Tangled Lines doesn't play Christmas music."

Piper gasped. "Oh my, whatever shall we do?" She stuck out her tongue.

"Now you're the incorrigible one."

Piper laughed. "Are you convinced we'll find a clue hidden under the shepherd's varnish?"

"Who knows, but I brought my scissors and tweezers. I'm prepared." She checked the rearview mirror and frowned. "There's a blue van behind us. Don't look back. Check the mirror."

The van trailed several car lengths behind. Piper groaned. "Can't tell if it's the same one, too far away."

"I'm losing them," Rosie said, stepping on the gas pedal. "Watch for coppers. I can't afford a ticket right now."

Piper gripped the handle on the door as Rosie sped down the road, careening around corners. "I think you lost them," she said after a glance in the mirror.

"Yes," Rosie squealed. A smile spread from ear to ear and she pumped her fist in the air. "I'll make a good detective yet."

Piper grinned, but she didn't loosen her grip on the door handle as Rosie swerved through Cranberry Harbor.

Piper shivered as she inserted the key in the lock of the empty academy. "Should we do this, Rosie? I don't have a good feeling."

"This is your academy, Piper. You can waltz in anytime you like. Give me those keys." She yanked open the door.

"Let's keep the lights off. Just in case," Piper said, locking the door.

"Creepy," Rosie said as they snuck down the dim hallway.

Piper unlocked the storage room door, and Rosie walked toward the table where they had left the broken nativity figures.

"Umm...Piper?"

"Hmm?"

"They're gone."

"What?" Piper ran to the middle of the room and stared at the empty table. "Where are they?"

Piper and Rosie separated to search.

"How did they get in??"

"Did an officer already collect the figures?" Rosie asked.

"I'll have to call Don."

Rosie stood in the middle of the room, her hands on her hips, turning slowly in a circle. She scratched her head and peeked underneath the table. "Piper, a clue."

Shards of wood from the broken nativity pieces lay under the table on top of a paper scrap. "I'm picking it up."

"Don't. You know what Chief Maxwell will say."

"If he wanted to find this little gem, he should have already come back to investigate." She spread the fragment on the table, gingerly patting the fragile paper.

Piper hovered over Rosie's shoulder.

"Turn on your phone light."

Piper pointed the light over the table.

"This is old," Rosie said. "What do you think?" She pointed to the elegant script flowing across the fragment.

"I'm clueless." Piper said. "German?"

"You're right. I think it *is* German," Rosie said. "Look here." She pointed to *das Lied*. Rosie scanned the paper, turning it in all directions. She held the piece up to the light. "Hmm…" Her eyes widened. "Remember when I was accidentally dusting inside Fergus's drawers?"

"Yes," Piper said. "And if you recall, I told you it was a terrible idea?"

Rosie tapped her chin, and her eyes narrowed. "If I remember correctly, the papers in one drawer looked similar. Maybe the writing was German too. I couldn't decipher any of the words."

Piper shook her head. "Rosie, what will I do with you?"

"Oh, come on, Piper. You're telling me you wouldn't have peeked?"

"No."

"Alright, Miss Goody Two-Shoes." Rosie tossed her curly hair over her shoulder. "Anyway. I didn't actually read much of anything. The beautiful handwriting resembled this." She tapped her finger on the table next to the paper. "Only one or two pages were English. The rest I didn't recognize."

Piper gasped as understanding crossed her face. "Rosie no. No way. We cannot go snooping around Fergus' house."

"Well, I can't sleep without taking a tiny little look-see inside those drawers."

"How will you get in? Do you have a key?"

"I do not have a key. And the question is not 'how will I get into Fergus' house?' The question is 'how will *we* get into Fergus' house?' We'll work out the details when we get there. You coming or not?"

Piper leaned against the table, her conscience warning her to call the police. But how would they connect the clues when Chief Maxwell took over?

"Fine. I'll go, but if anyone is there or I get the creeps, we're leaving."

"Yes!" Rosie said, pumping her fist. "I knew you'd see it my way."

"I can't see," Piper whispered when Rosie parked behind Fergus' house. "Why does night come at four o'clock in Wisconsin?"

"Don't complain. We're thankful for the cover tonight." Rosie hopped out of the car and gently closed the door. "I'll leave the doors unlocked in case we need to make a break for it."

The snow crunched underfoot, and the moon lit their path. "Try the front door?" Piper suggested.

"Let's go around back."

"You lead the way. I hope you know what you're doing." Piper trailed behind Rosie to the back of the house. Her heart pounded, and she shivered despite wearing her winter coat.

Rosie tugged on the sliding door they'd found open last night. "Locked," she whispered. "I'll try the kitchen door." They crunched through the snow to the kitchen, but no luck. Rosie turned and stared into Fergus' yard, pointing to a building in the far corner. She squinted. "A shed?"

"How am I supposed to know?"

"I found the papers in the room up there." Rosie pointed to a window above their heads. "If I can get up there, I can open the window and climb in."

"Rosie, this sounds like breaking and entering."

"Probably because it is. I'll work on an excuse while I'm rummaging for the papers. I work here, you know."

"Sure you do, but not in the middle of the night."

Rosie laughed. "It's not the middle of the night, silly. Come with me in case I need help. He must have a ladder in his shed."

"Our Sunday clothes don't lend themselves to tromping through the snow. Do you plan on climbing a ladder in your long skirt?"

"Don't be a party pooper." She stepped into the backyard, and Piper followed. Her heart pounded and the goosebumps on her arms multiplied, but she walked through the snow, ignoring the alarm bells jangling in her mind.

"How many miles long is this yard?" Piper huffed, her breath blowing out in a wisp. "The temperature is dropping. I can see my breath."

"Come on. We're on an adventure." Rosie tromped through the snow, and Piper stepped in Rosie's footprints to avoid filling her shoes with snow. She grumbled as her toes grew numb. *How does she talk me into these ridiculous ideas? If Dad finds out I did this, he will disown me.*

Rosie stopped near the building and pointed. "Well, well, well, what have we here?"

Piper trudged through the snow to catch up and gasped. "The nativity? What in the world?"

The missing nativity figures lay in a heap at the side of the shed. A disembodied Wise Man head stared up from the ground and Piper shivered. "Fergus didn't do this, did he?"

"I don't think so," Rosie said. "Help me." She bent and held the end of a long metal ladder.

"Good grief, Rosie. Who knew I needed to pump iron to keep up with you? My feet are numb."

"A few more minutes won't hurt you. Lift your end."

Piper lifted the end of the ladder and carried it to the house. "You owe me, Roosevelt Hale."

"You want to know what's in those papers as much as I do, Piper Haydn. Quit whining."

"You're not wrong, but I'm going to complain. I can't feel my feet."

Rosie leaned the ladder against the house and climbed the rungs.

"Hold on tight," Piper said. "Your shoes are wet."

"I am holding on tight. You hold the bottom," she called down to Piper.

Piper groaned. "If this thing falls, you know I can't stop it." She rested her foot on the bottom rung and held the sides of the ladder, muttering to herself. "This might be the most harebrained scheme Rosie ever dragged me into."

"I can hear you and we're in luck. Window's unlocked."

The red and green wool skirt disappeared into Fergus' window and Piper scanned the backyard. Her scalp prickled, and her clammy skin cooled in the frigid air. Her eye twitched and her heartbeat pounded in her ears. Stars twinkled in the inky black sky and Piper paused, whispering a long memorized psalm. "The heavens declare the glory of God." When she peered into the yard, the hair on the back of her neck stood. She frowned.

A light? An orange flicker near the shed shone for a moment and disappeared. Piper held her breath and bit her lip. Her hammering heart beat against her chest and chills rose on her arms.

Hurry, Rosie.

"Found 'em. Hold on. I'm coming down." Rosie's foot appeared out the window and the metal ladder clanked as she descended.

"You're loud enough to wake the dead," Piper complained.

Rosie's foot sunk into the snow at the bottom of the ladder, and she held up the stack of papers. "Well good, hopefully it wakes Fergus." She frowned. "We really need to find out if he pulled through."

"Put those in the car and help me drag this beast back to the shed, will you?"

Rosie ran to her car to deposit the papers, and Piper dragged the ladder across the yard. A flicker of light near the shed caught her eye, and she stopped. The orange light rose and tumbled across the yard. Piper's heart hammered and her lungs tightened. *No. No. No. This is not happening.*

Piper stood still when Rosie slammed the door and gritted her teeth. Whoever lurked behind the shed must have heard the racket. *Who am I kidding? They heard this entire ill-advised caper.*

Questioning her plan to return the ladder to the shed, she froze. *Should I run to the car or wait?*

"Hey, wait up, I'll help you," Rosie called, her footsteps crunching across the frozen ground.

"Rosie, someone's out there. By the shed," she whispered.

"What?" Rosie shrieked.

"Why don't you call attention to us, Rosie?" Piper said, staring into the yard for another flicker of light. "What should we do?"

"I don't know," Rosie hissed. "I can't see anything. We can't leave Fergus' ladder in the yard. If he survives, he'll have a fit."

A deep voice called from across the yard. "Fergus will have a fit about you climbing through his window, too."

Piper shook her arm free from Rosie's grip. "Back away," she whispered.

"No. I suggest you stand still," the voice said, stepping out of the shadows. A tall man appeared in front of them, the orange light glowing near his head.

"Cigarette," Piper whispered. "I should have known."

Rosie leaned in to whisper. "Who is that?"

"No idea."

"Ladies," the man said, stopping several feet away. "You've saved me from searching the house. If you'll hand over what you stole, I'll be on my way."

Rosie's chin rose, and she glared. "What are you talking about?"

His sardonic laugh floated across the yard. "I think you know. The papers. Hand them over."

"You don't know what I found. What are you looking for?" Rosie demanded.

He moved forward, and Piper stiffened as he reached out. "Cut the dumb chick act. I want the papers. Give them to me now and I'll forget to alert Fergus to your trespassing."

"You know Fergus?" Rosie asked. "And I'm not trespassing, by the way. I work here."

"Oh, really? Explains why you climbed a ladder into his second-floor window on a Sunday evening then? And yeah. You can say I know Fergus." The moonlight shone across the yard, but the man stood in the shadows, his face invisible.

"How do you know Fergus?" Piper asked.

Rosie stepped away from Piper, her hands on her hips. "Yeah. How do you know Fergus?"

The orange light flared and cigarette smoke floated around Piper. *He's moving closer.* Her heart pounded, and she searched for an escape. She couldn't use the ladder as a weapon—too heavy. Their purses sat in Rosie's car. Her frozen feet couldn't move fast enough to get away. She held a breath, trying to slow her heartbeat.

"How do you know Fergus?" Rosie demanded.

The man inched closer to their spot. "None of your business." He held out his hand. "Papers."

Clenching her chattering teeth, Piper took a step backward and whispered, "Run."

Rosie's ear-splitting scream split the air, and Piper jumped. Her blood pressure skyrocketed as adrenaline coursed through her system. She gripped her chest, hoping to avoid a heart attack.

Rosie sprinted to the car, with Piper close behind.

"Run, Rosie," Piper screamed. Her ballet flats slipped in the snow, and she lurched forward.

Rosie opened the car door. "Piper!" Her scream echoed across the yard.

"Call the police," Piper yelled, her breathing labored. Her lungs screamed for air, but the stranger had gained ground and his grunts filled her ears. Reaching deep into her reserves for a burst of energy, Piper ran, the dome light in Rosie's car lighting her path. Hope bubbled and relief warred with terror. *Almost there.* She breathed a sigh of relief, forcing her feet to move faster. *A few more steps and I'll...* Piper's foot slipped on a snow covered patch of ice. She slid into the splits and splatted to the ground, pain shooting through her legs.

"Rosie, go!" she screamed.

Rosie jumped from the car and ran to help Piper.

"No! Rosie, no! Get out of here. Go for help."

Her friend hesitated, but jumped in the car and roared out of the driveway. The taillights disappeared, and Piper breathed a prayer. *Oh Lord, I need you now.*

Pain overwhelmed Piper, and her hip throbbed. She rested her hand in the snow, trying to lift herself off the ground, and her fingers brushed a smooth rectangle. *Rosie's phone. No.*

Piper groaned, and her hand slid on the ice, dropping her into the snow.

"Now you've done it," the voice said as fingers dug into her shoulder.

Pain swirled, and she swayed as her head hit the ground.

When Piper opened her eyes, pain sliced through her. She groaned and blinked. "Where am I?"

"You're where you're going to stay until I get some answers," a deep voice said above her.

"Yeah," a woman chimed in.

Piper struggled to move into a sitting position and clenched her teeth. *I've broken something or badly sprained it.* "What answers do you want?" She frowned. "Are you responsible for the smashed pile of nativity figures we found at Fergus' shed?"

The man kicked her leg, and Piper's eyesight dimmed as nausea engulfed her.

"I'll ask the questions," he said. "Let's start with, who are you?"

"Who are *you*?" Piper blinked back tears.

The man's eyes flashed, and he leaned forward, baring his teeth. "Shut up."

Piper pressed her lips together and leaned back against the wall. *Is this the blue van?* She scanned the space, but pain clouded her vision and scrambled her thoughts. "Piper Haydn," she whispered, closing her eyes.

"Oh, this is good," the woman said. She clapped, each smack exploding in Piper's head.

"Why?" The man whipped his head around to the woman.

"The Haydns are rich."

Piper cracked an eye open and examined the woman. Long gray hair hung down her back in a ponytail loosely tied with a bright pink ribbon. She wore a baggy tattered brown sweater over a white turtleneck and jeans. The smile spreading across her face seemed out of place for the dire situation.

"Really?" the man voiced, shifting his gaze back to Piper. "How rich?"

"My family owns orchards and a fruit market here in Cranberry Harbor. How do I know my father's net worth?"

The man snorted and shifted in the seat. "Not broke then." He rubbed his hands together and licked his lips. "Perhaps we should write a little ransom note to dear old dad?"

Piper fought the fog, addling her brain. If the pain hadn't overwhelmed her and knocked all coherent thought from her head, she'd probably hyperventilate right now. But she couldn't think past the throbbing in her leg.

A cackle from the front of the van startled Piper's eyes open. *Is she the one I saw at the park last night?*

"Why are you staring at me like that?" The woman hit the man on the shoulder. "Ask her why she's staring at me like that."

He rubbed his shoulder. "Geez, Lynn. I don't know why she's staring at you like that." He glared at Piper. "Well?"

"Well, what?"

"Why are you staring at my aunt like that?"

Piper sighed at the ridiculous question. These people had kidnapped her, but now accused her of insulting them. "Your aunt?" She filed the little tidbit away to tell Chief Maxwell if she ever saw him again. Her stomach dropped. *He's going to read me the riot act. Why didn't I listen?* "Who are you?"

He nudged her with his foot, and pain shot through her leg. Her vision dimmed. She gasped, trying to keep her eyes open. "Please don't." Tears pooled in the corner of her eyes. "I need to see a doctor. Set me on the side of the road. I won't say anything."

The man laughed. "Hear her, Lynn? She won't say anything."

"She's the type to run straight to the police. Probably dating one of them," the woman said.

Piper straightened her spine and glared. "I am *not* dating a police officer."

The woman smirked. "Hmm. She's mighty defensive about not dating the police. I'd say she is."

The man rested his hands on his knees and leaned over to Piper. "Listen, I don't want to hurt you. But I need the papers your friend stole. What was on them?"

"I didn't see anything," Piper said, hating the whine creeping into her voice. Her leg throbbed and her frozen feet prickled when she moved. At least they had the heater running, but Piper's teeth chattered. "How do you expect me to answer when I don't know?"

The man clenched his jaw. "Oh, you know. You and your friend wouldn't break into my father's house just to be nosy."

Piper frowned. "Your father? Fergus is your father?" She stared at the woman. "You're his sister-in-law?" *Had Rosie mentioned her name?*

The woman's nostrils flared. "You're a genius. Spill it. What's on the papers your friend stole?"

"How am I supposed to know?"

The man pointed to the front, and her captors climbed into their seats. Piper strained to hear their conversation, but he cranked the volume on the radio. She leaned her head on the side of the van. *Well, God. I messed up. Please send help.*

"The manuscript...."

"Need to find..."

Bits of conversation floated back to Piper. She slowed her breathing to eavesdrop, but the snippets of conversation added to the swirling fog in her brain. *Surely Rosie called the police by now. Help is on the way. It has to be.* Her eyes closed, and she dozed.

A roaring motor startled Piper awake, and the floor underneath her vibrated. The van sped through the night, bumping over ruts in the road, jostling her leg. Pain throbbed with every bump and she bit her lip to hold back tears. She whispered a Bible verse to calm her fear. *What time I am afraid I will trust in you.*

She hadn't heard enough of their conversation to answer her questions. Had they destroyed the nativity figures? What did they want? Why was Fergus involved? *Was* Fergus involved?

"Rosie, send help," she whispered.

"What did you say?" the man yelled.

"Sleeping Beauty is awake," the woman said, turning to leer at Piper. The woman's beady eyes sparkled, and she grinned.

"Hey," the man yelled, turning around. "Hey you back there. You need to..."

"Everett!" the woman yelled.

Piper tumbled through the back of the van like a rag doll. Her arms and legs bobbing as if she weighed nothing. When her head hit the floor, darkness swirled and her fears disappeared.

Chapter 7

The night is peaceful all around you. Close your eyes, let sleep surround you.

Sunday Evening

Rosie screamed when Piper slid on the ice. "No!" Her heart pounded, and she jumped out of the car, running to her friend.

"No! Rosie, no! Get out of here. Get help."

Rosie hesitated, but returned to the car and roared out of the driveway. Leaving Piper behind felt like a sin, but she had to go for help. If she got out of the car and the lunatic kidnapped both of them, no one would ever know what happened.

She stomped on the gas pedal, praying for the tires to find dry ground—not ice. With one hand on the steering wheel and the other patting the seat in search of her phone, she stared at the road in front of her, praying for smooth sailing. "Where is my phone? Don't tell me I dropped it."

Her heart pounded in her ears and her hands shook as she gripped the wheel. If Piper hadn't fallen on the ice in front of the car, Rosie would have driven straight into that man.

"Why? Why? Why?" she screamed, hitting the steering wheel. "What's in those papers worth kidnapping someone for?" She flipped the headlights to bright and raced down the road into town, praying she'd speed past an officer waiting to fulfill their ticket quota for the day. "Pull me over," she begged as she sped into town. "The chief is going to yell at me. Why do I get these stupid ideas? We shouldn't have gone over there. Piper didn't want to, but did I listen? Noooooooo. Roosevelt Hale had to drag her best friend into a kidnapper's lair and now a beast has captured her."

Tears stung Rosie's eyes, but hope swelled in her heart when the city lights of Cranberry Harbor twinkled in front of her. "Now, where's an officer when I need one?" Her eyes darted around the road and side streets. "Come on, pull me over."

She jammed the gas pedal to the floor, praying she wouldn't plow into a pedestrian. Her heart hammered in her chest and tears burned her eyes.

Red and blue lights circled behind her, and a siren wailed. Tears of relief poured down her cheeks as she pulled to the side of the road. "Oh, thank God," she whispered. "Please don't be Chief Maxwell."

The officer tapped her window, and Rosie groaned.

"Miss Hale?" Chief Maxwell stood at her door, his eyes blazing.

"He kidnapped Piper," she gasped, unable to catch her breath. "Hurry."

The chief's eyes widened, and he leaned into her window. "Please step out of the car. Keep your hands where I can see them."

Rosie popped the door open and stepped out. Frigid wind blew across her face, and she wiped her cheeks before the tears froze. "He's got her. She fell on the ice and he nabbed her."

"Who?"

"That man," she wailed. Sobs shook her, and she shivered.

"What man? Where?"

"At Fergus'," Rosie cried, blowing out a ragged breath.

"You were at Fergus'? Doing what?" His eyes narrowed. "I *told* you to stay away." He ran a hand through his hair and clenched his jaw.

"The papers, and the nativity figures, and..."

The chief held up a hand. "We'll talk about the why later. Did you see their vehicle? What did he look like?"

Rosie answered his questions as sirens wailed, the lights growing closer. "I can't describe much, but Piper noticed a blue van at the park last night and one sped past us on our way to carol at Fergus' house."

Chief Maxwell directed the officers over the radio. "Anderson and Roth, check out Fergus Standerwick's place. All other squads, we're searching for a blue van model unknown. Spread out and report anything you find. I'm heading to the station."

He leaned in Rosie's window. "Follow me to the station. Do not speed."

Rosie's heart raced and tears streamed down her cheeks. She'd expected relief at finding help for Piper, but the concern in Chief Maxwell's eyes assured her she wasn't overreacting. She pulled onto the street behind his squad car. Taking deep breaths to calm herself, she clutched the steering wheel and prayed.

"What were you thinking?" Chief Maxwell slammed his notebook on the table and dropped into the seat across from Rosie.

Rosie twisted her hands in her lap and sniffled. "We were investigating," she whispered.

"Investigating what?"

"A clue." She reached for a tissue and blew her nose.

His eyes flashed, but he lowered his voice. "Miss Hale, I instructed you and Miss Haydn to stay out of the investigation. I can't understand your thought process, but as you have discovered...again...you need to leave investigating to the professionals. Start at the beginning." Flipping open his notebook, he held a pen over the page and stared at Rosie.

"We didn't intend to get in your way. But the other day, we examined the nativity figures in Piper's storeroom." She grimaced at his raised eyebrows and stern face.

"Go on."

"When we examined the broken figures, we discovered handwriting on an old piece of paper underneath the finish of the shepherd."

The chief nodded.

"I found similar papers at his house and convinced Piper to go to Fergus' with me."

He cleared his throat and tapped the pen on the notebook. "And how did you find these papers in the first place?"

"I work at Fergus's you know? I found them when I was accidentally dusting inside the dresser drawers in a room upstairs."

His eyebrow rose. "Accidentally?"

Heat flooded her cheeks. "Well, accidentally on purpose."

"What did you find on these papers?"

"Nothing, because most of the writing was another language. The handwriting was old-fashioned script, similar to the paper under the shepherd."

"Why didn't you call me?"

"Would you have listened?"

"Did you give me a chance to listen, Miss Hale?" He leaned back in his chair. "What convinced you to break into Fergus' tonight?"

"I wanted to peek at the papers and see if I was right." Her voice caught, and she stared at her hands. "It's my fault for talking Piper into going. She didn't want to."

"Do you have a key to Mr. Standerwick's home?"

Rosie wiped the corner of her eye and whispered, "No."

He dropped his pencil and leaned back in his chair. "Unbelievable."

"Is Fergus alright?"

"You know I can't disclose Mr. Standerwick's medical condition, Rosie."

A grin spread across her face.

"What?"

"You said he has a medical condition. He's still alive."

Chief Maxwell waved his pen. "Back to the story. What happened after you broke in?"

"Oh!" Rosie yelled. "The papers are on my front seat."

He stepped into the hall, calling for an officer. Rosie waited at the table, her heart pounding. *Help them find Piper. Please, God.*

"What happened next?" he said, returning to the table.

Rosie filled him in on the lurking man, their run across the frozen back yard, Piper's fall, and Rosie's escape. "I dropped my phone somewhere out there. I couldn't even call you." A tear trickled down her cheeks and the chief slid the box of tissues across the table.

"I shouldn't need to tell you this, Miss Hale, but there's a reason we want you to leave the investigating to us. Neither one of you should face this kind of danger."

Rosie plucked a tissue from the box and sobbed. "I know. But I didn't think you'd listen."

A knock at the door interrupted Rosie's sobs. The officer entered, placing a stack of papers on the table.

Chief Maxwell frowned and flipped through the sheets. "I'm not sure what I'm looking at here. What's the link between these papers and the broken nativity?"

Rosie pointed to the flowing script on the top page. "It's the same writing as the paper underneath the shepherd."

"We'll find someone who can read it." He flipped a page and glanced up. "This one is music." Tapping the paper, he moved the pile across the table.

"Miss Hale, I'm going to send you home for the night. I'm ordering you to stay far away from my investigation. Do you understand?"

"Yes, sir."

He smiled and patted her hand. "Look at me, Rosie."
She wiped her cheek and blinked away a tear.
"We'll find her."

CHAPTER 8

Sleep, sleep, sleep. 'Tis the eve of our Saviour's birth.

Monday Morning

Piper faked sleep as she peeked around the interior of the windowless cargo van through a slit in her eyelids. The man drove, and the woman rode in the passenger seat, snoring.

Her leg throbbed, and pain squeezed her head. Had they driven all night? She couldn't remember. She didn't remember falling asleep either and wondered why she lay sprawled on the floor. For now, she'd keep her eyes closed and listen for clues.

As the sun rose, Piper tried to peek through the windshield without alerting her captors. If she moved, they'd know she was awake. *Is the sun ahead of us? Are we moving east? Where are we going?* She strained to see the road, but could only glimpse the sky.

The woman snorted and sat up. Piper held her breath and lay still.

"Good thing you didn't crack this up when you plowed into the snowbank last night. Running a little rough though, huh?" She punched his arm.

He nodded. "It's running fine. Almost there."

Piper concentrated, trying to gather pieces of the conversation, but dozed as the van rocked and her headache escalated.

The van shuddered, and a door slammed. Piper opened her eyes and sat up, her stiff muscles begging her to lie still. *Where'd they go?* She crawled to the front seat and gasped. The keys dangled in the ignition and her heart pounded. Could she drive off and leave them behind? But where were they? Would her leg hold up?

She leaned on the seat and struggled to peek out the windshield. *A gas station.* The hazy windows obscured movement inside. Gritting her teeth, she dragged herself into the driver's seat and cranked the key. The van roared to life, and she pressed on the gas pedal, but white hot pain jolted up her leg and her head swam. Tears blurred her vision, and she slammed the steering wheel. "I can't drive like this," she cried. A tear rolled down her cheek as her chance for escape slipped away.

The door of the gas station slammed opened and her captors ran out. Piper's eyes widened, and she reached for the lock button. Her heart pounded in her chest. *What do I do? Did they have a weapon?* Crouching in the back of the van wouldn't help if they had a gun.

Her captors yelled, waving their arms as they ran across the parking lot. Piper's heart pounded. The woman reached for the door, yanking on the handle and banging.

"This idiot locked us out," she screeched.

The man sprinted to the driver's door, tugged the handle, and locked eyes with her. "Open the door!" he ordered, his eyes bulging and his face flushing.

Piper leaned forward, blasting the horn.

"Stop it," the woman yelled.

The man disappeared, and Piper craned her neck to keep track of him. The back door opened and Piper screamed. Tears rolled down her cheeks. "No." She clenched the steering wheel as the man barreled through the van, screaming profanities.

He reached forward and yanked her arm. Piper watched the gas station as he drug her from the seat. A man stood at the door, his mouth open. *Please call for help.*

Face down on the floor of the van, Piper lay still as the man swung the door open for his aunt. She jumped into the passenger seat, cursing, and the man raced onto the road, tires squealing as he sped away.

"Now you've done it," he said. "I *told* you we didn't want to hurt you. But your little trick back there changes the plans. All I wanted was the papers your friend stole. But no. You had to get smart."

Tears stung Piper's eyes, and she rolled onto her side. *Smart girls don't let their best friend talk them into breaking and entering.*

"Have her call her friend and arrange a hand-off," the woman suggested.

"No. Too risky."

"What are you going to do?"

"Will you shut up? I'm thinking."

The woman huffed. "Fine way to talk to your aunt."

"I'm stressed out alright?"

You're stressed out? What about me? Piper lay on the floor, jostling as the van sped down the road. *I'm in so much trouble.*

Piper lost track of time. Had they been driving for minutes or hours? When the van slowed, Piper tensed, listening for noises to help identify her whereabouts.

The back door opened, and the man reached into the van, tugging her to the edge. "Stand up." He barked.

Her feet throbbed, and her knees buckled, dropping her into the snow.

"Get up," he yelled, yanking her arm and jerking her to her feet. "Get inside. Move." He pointed down the path to a cabin.

Piper's heart pounded, and the hair on the back of her neck stood up. *Every thriller starts with a cabin in the woods.* She hobbled down the walkway, the stabbing pain in her leg screaming at every step.

He nudged her from behind and squeezed her arm.

"This is unnecessary, you know. I can't run away," Piper said, jerking her arm from his hand.

He shoved her forward. "Quit talking."

"Yeah, quit talking."

He scowled. "I'll handle this."

"You will not shout orders at me, Everett."

"Lynn," he roared.

Frowning, the woman trudged to the cabin and opened the door.

Piper examined the large open room of the cabin from a chair where he'd shoved her. A massive fieldstone fireplace rose to the vaulted ceiling, and a stack of logs sat near the hearth. Plush couches lined the walls and a large table at the center held a stack of games, a vase of flowers, and a pile of books. A grand piano in the corner held sheet music. Piper blinked. *What is this place? Certainly doesn't seem like a serial killer lair.*

"Nice place, huh?" the man said. "I told you we don't want to hurt you. But your little stunt means I can't trust you."

"Where are we?" Piper massaged her temples.

"My cabin. Built with my inheritance from mother."

"Was Fergus' wife your sister?" Piper asked the woman.

The woman's eyes filled with tears. "She was the best sister ever." She wiped her eyes and glared at Piper. "What are we going to do about her, Everett? You can't keep her here forever."

Piper's heart pounded, and she glanced back and forth between them. In the light of day, the kidnappers seemed less threatening—almost normal. But the bruises on her arms and her throbbing body told another story. "Can I have some ice?" She shifted in her chair to ease the ache in her leg.

The woman disappeared and returned with ice cubes in a plastic bag, tossing them in Piper's direction.

Piper grimaced and strained to reach the ice from the floor. She grunted and pinched the edge of the bag, biting her lip as she settled in the chair with the ice against her side.

Everett sat on the coffee table, drumming his fingers on his knees. "Listen. We never meant for any of this to happen."

Piper frowned. "Then why were you lurking in the shadows in Fergus' backyard? Why did you drag me into your van? Kidnapping is illegal, you know."

He ran his fingers through his hair and blew out a breath. His eyes clouded, and he stared out the plate-glass window. "We came to talk to father—to explain. But he wouldn't listen. He…"

"Everett," Lynn warned.

"It's no use. We're in too deep." He stood, towering over Piper, and leaned forward, jabbing his finger in her face. "This is your fault."

"Are you accusing me of this mess?"

"Are you stupid? Yes, I'm accusing you. What was written on the papers your friend stole?

Tears stung Piper's eyes. Her painful leg throbbed and her numb feet tingled as they warmed. She stared at the fireplace. "I told you I didn't see them." She reached up to brush a tear from her cheek, hating how feeble she appeared. "Can I have a blanket? Please?"

The woman glared and whipped an afghan from the back of the couch, tossing the blanket on Piper's lap before turning away.

"I don't believe you." Everett shoved the games off the table, pieces scattering across the room.

Piper flinched. "You were there. You saw the whole thing. My friend went in, found the papers, climbed down the ladder and you accosted us."

"Drop the innocent act. You trespassed."

"*I* trespassed? What about you?" Piper sputtered.

"Fergus knew we were there," the woman said. "Besides, he's family. You're not."

"Seems odd to me for family to lurk in the shadows, casing his house."

Everett jumped to his feet and flailed his hands in the air. "Enough. What are you doing?" He whipped around to his aunt.

"She's cold. I'm bringing her tea."

Piper reached for the tea and wrapped her hands around the teacup, soaking in the warmth. She leaned her head back on the chair, closing her eyes, peering at her captors through the slit in her eyelids.

The woman jerked her head toward Piper and pointed to the cup.

The man mouthed, "Oh."

She examined the mug of cloudy yellow tea, remembering the empty teacup at Fergus' house. A chill slithered up her spine.

She opened her eyes and set the mug on the table. "Why don't you tell me why you want those papers?"

"No." His lip curled, and Lynn rested her hand on his arm.

"My brother-in-law is an impossible man, and this is not your concern." She scowled at her nephew. "What are we planning to do with her?" She jerked her thumb toward Piper.

"Leave it to me," he said, and marched out, slamming the door behind him.

"Listen," the woman said to Piper. "I'm bringing my things in from the van. No funny business."

Piper pointed to her swollen leg. "Where do you think I'm going?"

The woman huffed and walked to the door.

"Hey, you don't need to follow him," Piper called. "You can make your own decisions."

The woman turned and stared at Piper. "Shut up."

Piper leaned forward to peek out the window, but a log beam blocked her vision. She turned, scanning the cabin. Her heart raced and a spring of hope bubbled. *A phone on the kitchen wall.* Her heart hammered. *What if my leg gives out, or she comes back?* She couldn't let this opportunity slip through her fingers. She stood as quickly as her swollen limbs allowed and hobbled to the kitchen.

Pain tore through her, but she pressed on. *Oh, please, God, help me,* she prayed, clutching the backs of chairs and the counter as she bumbled her way to the phone. *Almost there.* She lurched forward, snatching the receiver, and stabbed at the numbers on the phone, hoping she hadn't punched in the wrong numbers.

"Bear Lake County dispatch."

Her voice caught and hear heart pounded. "I need…" she whispered.

The cabin door opened and Piper gasped, slamming the phone down. She spun to the counter, knocking a jar over as she fumbled for a glass. Her knees shook, and she stifled a scream.

"Hey! What are you doing?" the woman yelled from the front door.

Piper swallowed to steady her voice. "My hands are sticky." She held them up in the air, willing them to stop trembling. "I needed to wash."

The woman clenched her jaw and stepped into the kitchen. Her eyes darted across the space, and she scowled at Piper. "Wash up. Go sit down." She spun around, scanning the kitchen, then stared at Piper.

Piper's hands trembled as she hobbled back to the living room. *Was my call long enough for them to find me?* She settled in the chair and tucked the blanket over her. Thankfully, the ice pack offered slight relief.

"You hungry? Finish your tea?" the woman called from the kitchen.

Piper's hand shook as she took the tea, and the cup clattered against the saucer. "I'm not hungry," she said. She closed her eyes, remembering the face the woman had made when handing her the tea and the teacup next to Fergus' table. Piper raised the cup to her mouth, but shifted toward the fireplace to hide her next move. She tipped the mug and spilled hot liquid onto the cushion of her chair. Perhaps the tea was fine, but Piper had sufficient reason to distrust the ill-tempered woman.

The front door slammed open. "Lynn! There's a car out there. Keeps driving up and down the road." His eyes darted around the room. "We need to leave. Pick up your stuff."

"I dragged everything in here ten minutes ago," she whined.

"Hurry," he said, snatching up his bag and reaching for Piper. He jerked her from the chair and tossed her over his shoulder. His shoulder bones slammed into her stomach, forcing the air out of her lungs in a whoosh.

She gasped for breath as he ran to the van. He slid on the icy path, jostling her painful leg. Alarms and bright colors swirled through her head and she fought black clouds churning at the corners of her mind. When pain sucked her into an abyss, she surrendered. Evil won.

Chapter 9

Dream, dream, dream of the joyous day to come.

Monday Afternoon

Quinn Harper clicked off a call and yelled into the police station. "Chief! Come quick." The buzz of officers working the case halted, and all eyes turned to Quinn.

Chief Maxwell ran around the corner. "Quinn?"

"Bear Lake County called. They received a hang-up call from a cabin deep in the woods. Their department sent a squad to check it out."

Chief Maxwell squared his shoulders. "How far is Bear Lake County?"

Quinn tapped on the keyboard and studied the monitor. "Map says ninety miles."

"Who's going with me? Might be a lead."

Deputy Gunther stood. "I'll go, chief."

Will nodded. "Collect your gear. We'll leave in five. And Quinn, call me on the radio if anything else comes in. You gave them my number?"

Quinn nodded. "Will do. And yes, they have your number."

"Hold down the fort."

"Yes, sir. I hope it's her," she whispered.

"Me too, Quinn," the chief said, hurrying to his office.

Traveling down the highway, Will resisted the urge to speed. The dry roads permitted him to push the speed limit, but he didn't want to take chances. Winter roads hid icy spots and the thought of veering off into a snowy ditch gave him a chill. They had no time to waste.

Gunther cleared his throat. "Think it's Miss Haydn?"

"Hope so."

He grinned. "You got something going on with her?"

Chief Maxwell stared at the road ahead. "I'd like to say yes, but Miss Haydn has expressly conveyed her disinterest."

"Too bad. You two look great together."

"Thanks, Gunther, but a good relationship might need a little more than looking good together."

"I know, but I can't help saying it. Why don't you ask her out again?"

Will tapped his finger on the steering wheel. "Have to find her first."

"Good point,"

"Playing matchmaker since you've settled down?" Will smiled as he teased the officer.

"Hey, happiness is a great thing." Gunther grinned. "What do you make of those papers Miss Hale brought in?"

"I flipped through them and several sheets appear to be music, although I am unsure of what the music is or how this ties in to Piper's abduction. Doubt we can use anything as evidence. I spoke with a professor from UW Madison. She agreed to examine the papers and give us an idea of their significance."

"Update on Fergus this morning?"

Chief Maxwell shook his head. "No. Remind me to call when we get back. Things weren't looking good last night, but I'm praying he pulls through."

The radio crackled. "Squad 1, please respond," Quinn's voice echoed through the speaker.

"Squad 1."

"Bear Lake County reports an unfolding situation. Young woman held hostage by a man and an older woman. Blue van on premises. No identification yet."

"Squad 1. En route to the scene." He released the talk button and said, "Let's go." He stepped on the gas pedal, and the cruiser sped down highway 41.

Rosie paced in her living room, ignoring the paint and paper she'd set out to finish the labels for the Christkindlmarket. She couldn't concentrate. "Why did I talk you into going with me, Piper? I'm too old to be foolish." She wrung her hands and dropped onto the couch, burrowing underneath an orange and brown crocheted afghan. "Here's the thing, God. I don't mean to do stupid things. Piper is a stupendous friend. She humors me and my harebrained ideas even when she disagrees. Please, lead the police to her. Please, let them find her in time."

She reached for her tablet and searched her music app for Handel's *Messiah*. "I'll pray for Piper while I listen," she whispered, and drifted into a restless sleep as the comforting strains of "He shall feed his flock" floated through the room.

The Haydn family gathered, waiting for news of Piper's whereabouts. Jack Haydn sat at the dining room table, his phone nearby. He stared out the window, drumming his fingers on the table, his jaw tight.

Asher and Landon ran circles around the room until their mother shooed them away. "Grandpa needs to concentrate. Go help Glammy in the kitchen," Emily said. She turned to Braden, the baby on her hip. "Anything?"

"No," he whispered. "But Dad's on top of it. He'll let us know."

Chase burst through the door, waving his phone. "Did you see the Tattler?"

Sarah stepped into the room, wiping her hands on an apron. The family crowded Chase, peering over his shoulder.

"Read it out loud, son," Jack said.

Chase cleared his throat and read.

"Sunday evening, two 'upstanding' citizens of Cranberry Harbor broke into the home of the very well respected Fergus Standerwick. The women gained access by using a tall ladder and entering an upper-story window. One suspect removed valuables from the home. Citizens of Cranberry Harbor, will you tolerate this behavior, or will you insist the police do their job? Is Chief Maxwell capable of leading the force? Is our police department in the back pocket of Jack Haydn? We want to know. Call the mayor. Make your voice heard today."

"We need to make our voices heard about this hack piece," Jack said, pointing at Chase's screen.

Braden scowled. "Who has information not released to the public?"

"Have you heard from Rosie?" Chase asked.

Braden stared.

"What? You're not blaming Rosie, are you? We all know Piper is stubborn when she gets an idea."

"Sarah, will you call Roosevelt, please?" Jack asked. "Invite her to join us."

The Haydns settled around the table, waiting for the phone to ring.

The ringing phone roused Rosie from her nap. "Hello?"

"Roosevelt, darling, we'd like you to join us while we wait for news."

"You're not angry?" Her voice trembled. "It's all my fault."

"No, honey, it isn't your fault," Sarah said. "Our daughter has a mind of her own. She may have protested, but we know she wouldn't have gone with you if she didn't want to."

Rosie wiped her eyes. "Thank you," she whispered.

"You haven't been sitting there alone worrying, have you?"

"Maybe."

"I'm sending Chase to gather you. Unless you'd rather drive?"

"You can send him over." She swallowed over the lump in her throat. "Thank you, Mrs. Haydn."

"You're welcome. See you soon."

Rosie exhaled all the pent-up worry she'd held since the beast had kidnapped her best friend. Orchestra music floated through the room, and Rosie frowned. She paused the music and dragged the slider back to listen again. "Let all the angels of God..." blared through the speaker. She tapped her lip and closed her eyes, straining to picture the papers she'd swiped from the dresser drawer. When she was 'accidentally' dusting the drawers while working for Fergus, she had read those words.

Rosie clicked off the music app and stood. No use. She couldn't remember. "Why didn't I take a peek last night?" she asked herself and rushed to change before Chase arrived.

Tugging a comb through her curls, she peeked in the mirror. Deep circles lined her red-rimmed eyes. "Ugh. What a mess." She slipped into a vintage red polyester shift dress trimmed with white piping.

She dug through the basket on her dresser searching for a piece of jewelry to accent the stiff bright red fabric and chose an enamel holly and berries stick pin. Her crush on Chase Haydn wasn't going anywhere—at least not as long as he remained immature and involved in questionable activities. Her perfect outfit couldn't hide the effects of restless sleep, but at least she wouldn't resemble a troll around Chase.

She stepped into white patent leather boots as the doorbell rang. "Coming," she hollered and took one last look.

"What possessed you to go to Fergus' place?" Chase asked as he drove through Cranberry Harbor.

"It's a little complicated, and your parents want the same answers. Can I explain all at once?"

"Whatever. You think Piper is alive and well?"

Rosie shuddered. "If she's not, I'll never forgive myself."

"Hey," Chase said, reaching to pat her hand. "Don't be hard on yourself. You know Piper wouldn't have gone if she didn't want to."

"Are you sure? I talked her into glamping in Door County. We all know what happened there."

Chase grimaced. "Apparently, your powers of persuasion are second to none. Looking a little rough, my friend. Did you have trouble sleeping?"

Rosie elbowed Chase in the stomach.

"Hey," he said. "Why'd you elbow me?"

"You never tell a lady she looks horrible. How rude."

"In my defense, I used the word rough."

"Still." Rosie huffed.

Chase turned into the broad driveway leading to the Haydn home and parked his Tesla near the front door. He walked around and opened the car door for Rosie.

She grinned. "Wow. You *can* be a gentleman, huh?"

He bowed. "At your service, madam." He held his arm out to her, and she slipped her hand inside his elbow.

"Rosie's here," he hollered when they stepped into the house.

"In the dining room," Jack Haydn called.

The family gathered around the table. An untouched plate of cookies sat in the middle, and the adults held mugs of coffee.

"Would you like a latte, Rosie?" Sarah Haydn rose from her chair. "Vanilla?"

"Yes, please." Rosie slid into the seat next to Emily.

"Roosevelt, when my wife returns, I'd like to hear all about the caper you and Piper Grace went on last night. Seems I'm missing some details."

Rosie gulped. "Yes, sir."

Sarah set a mug in front of Rosie. "I got this one when we went to the top of the Burj Khalifa. When did we visit Dubai, Jack? Three years ago?"

"I believe so, darling. Have a seat. Rosie wants to fill us in on what she and our daughter were doing breaking into Fergus' last night. Right, Rosie?" Jack cleared his throat.

Sarah's eyes widened, and she settled into the chair next to her husband. She reached across the table and squeezed Rosie's hand. "Yes, please fill us in."

"First, may I ask if you've heard anything about Fergus?"

Jack Haydn cleared his throat. "No, and it's not for lack of trying."

Rosie nodded and twisted her fingers in her lap. Her cheeks burned, and she dropped her chin to her chest. "I know this will strike you as crazy, but it made perfect sense to me in the moment."

"Go ahead." He leaned back in his chair, his arms folded across his chest.

"You heard about the damaged nativity figures we discovered at the academy?"

Jack nodded.

"We went back to investigate, and we found a paper with beautiful handwriting underneath the varnish. We picked at the finish, hoping we could decipher the words, but we ran out of time. Piper had to get to the park for caroling." Rosie glanced around the table at Piper's family, and a lump rose in her throat. "We all know what happened to Fergus?"

"Yes," Sarah said.

"After we left here Sunday, we went back to the academy to get a better look at the shepherd. We knew Chief Maxwell planned to send an officer to collect the rest of the set on Monday, and we wanted to search for clues before he took away our opportunity." She frowned and picked at her fingernail.

Emily reached over and patted Rosie's arm, encouraging her with a smile. "What did you find?"

Rosie sucked in a breath to calm her quivering lip. "While we were looking, I remembered papers I saw in a drawer at Fergus'. The handwriting seemed similar."

Jack leaned forward. "How did you find papers in his drawers? Were you organizing?"

"No, sir, I was dusting," Rosie said, focusing on her hands in her lap. She cleared her throat. "Inside his drawers."

"Dusting? Or snooping?" he asked.

Pink flooded her cheeks. "Snooping." She rushed on. "The paper underneath the finish on the shepherd had the same fancy old-fashioned writing I noticed on the papers in his drawer." She examined her hands in her lap and looked up with a weak smile. "I talked Piper into going to Fergus' with me to look. I was hoping a door would be unlocked, but..."

"How did you get in?" Braden asked.

"We dragged a ladder from the back shed." Heat flooded her cheeks. "I know I shouldn't have. We were still wearing our church clothes, for crying out loud."

Sarah reached across the table and held out her hand to Rosie.

She squeezed Mrs. Haydn's hand and let out a ragged breath.

"Go ahead," Sarah said.

Her eyes filled with tears, and she blinked. "I climbed through the unlocked window and found the papers easy-peasy. We planned to examine them over at Piper's. I picked up my end of the ladder to help Piper drag it back to the shed. And then the trouble started." She stopped and rubbed her eyes. "When we got halfway to the shed, a man was lurking in the shadows. I think he'd been watching the whole time."

"Who was it?" Chase demanded.

Rosie ignored him and continued. "We dropped the ladder and ran to the car. I made it, but Piper slipped on the ice and he nabbed her."

"Why didn't you call for help right away?" Sarah asked.

"I lost my phone in the snow." Tears spilled down her cheeks. "When I jumped out of the car to help her, she screamed at me to leave and get help. I didn't know what to do. If I stayed, he might have abducted both of us and no one would ever know."

Emily patted Rosie's arm. "You did the right thing. At least we have an idea what happened. If he had abducted both of you, we'd be clueless."

"What about the papers?" Jack asked.

"By the time I got pulled over for speeding and told Chief Maxwell everything, I forgot about them. When everything settled down, I turned them over. They're at the police station." A sob overtook her, and she wailed. "I didn't even get a peek, and now Piper is missing, and it's all my fault."

"Listen, Rosie. No one is blaming you. Piper is an adult, and she went willingly with you." Jack pinched the bridge of his nose and blew out a breath. "I want you and my daughter to obey the chief.

Investigating crimes is for the professionals." Jack Haydn peered over his glasses at Rosie. His gaze stern.

"Yes, sir," she whispered.

Sarah reached for the empty mugs. "Anyone need a refill? I can't sit any longer." She collected the mugs and stood.

Jack's phone rang, and everyone stilled. "Jack Haydn here. Yes. Really? Wonderful. We're on our way. Thank you."

He set the phone down, and his voice shook. "They found her."

The dining room erupted in shouts and cheers. Sarah collapsed into her chair, tears rolling down her cheeks. "Praise God," she repeated over and over.

All the fears she'd held at bay during the past hours crashed over Rosie, and she sobbed. Emily reached over and hugged her. "Everything's going to be fine, Rosie. She's safe."

Rosie nodded into Emily's shoulder. "I'm getting your sweater wet," she murmured.

Emily leaned back and laughed. "Don't worry about my sweater." She turned to the room. "Who's going to pick up our girl?"

Jack raised his hand. "She's in the hospital in Bear Lake County."

The room fell silent, and then everyone spoke at once.

"Is she alright?"

"What happened?"

"What's going on?"

"Is she hurt?"

"Is Auntie Piper sick?" Asher asked from the doorway. A tear trickled down his check.

Jack turned and held out a hand to his grandson. "We don't know, Asher, but we'll find out soon. Don't worry." He stood. "Let's stop to pray, then we'll decide who's going." He reached out to Sarah, and the family joined hands around the table.

"Father, thank you for finding Piper. Please hold her close and keep her safe. If she has injuries, please guide the hands of the medical professionals. Help us trust you and know she's held in the palm of your mighty hand. We ask for healing and justice. Amen."

Amens echoed around the table.

Emily stood, holding baby Zeke. "You go. The boys and I will stay here and wait for news. Call me if you hear anything." She stood on tiptoe and kissed Braden on the cheek.

Rosie nodded to Emily as she settled in the backseat of the Haydn's black Cadillac. The boys huddled around their mom in the doorway, waving as Jack backed out of the driveway and sped toward Piper.

Piper lay on the hospital bed, her leg encased in a cast. A mound of pillows elevated her foot, and medication had finally eased her pain. Officers surrounded her bed, asking questions. She answered as honestly as she could, but as the medication took effect, she mumbled and her eyelids drooped.

"My patient needs a break," a nurse said, stepping to the side of Piper's bed. She squeezed Piper's hand and fluffed the pillows under her head and leg.

The officers filed out of the room, and Piper closed her eyes to rest before Chief Maxwell arrived. She cringed, anticipating the ear blistering lecture he'd deliver, but as she drifted to sleep, she thought of his brown eyes and deep voice and smiled.

When Rosie and the Haydn family arrived at the hospital, they found Chief Maxwell huddled in the lobby with the officers from Bear Lake County. He gestured for the Haydns to join the circle. Rosie held back, watching the group, longing desperately for news of her friend.

Chase turned and signaled to Rosie. She raised an eyebrow and pointed to herself.

"Come on," he mouthed, stepping aside to make space for her in the circle.

"Miss Hale," Chief Maxwell nodded. "These officers are filling us in."

Rosie listened to the officer speaking. She'd missed part of the story, but she'd catch up later.

"We have more questions for Miss Haydn, but the nurse asked us to give her a break. The pain medication made her drowsy."

"What's her condition?" Sarah asked in a whisper. She clutched Jack's arm and her eyes watered.

The officer flipped a page in his notebook. "Miss Haydn has a bruised hip, and a hairline fracture on her femur. She stated she fell on the ice while attempting to escape. The suspects didn't cause the injury. She has bruising from the suspect snatching her. Overall, she's stable, but you'll need to request specifics from her doctor."

"Thank God," Sarah Haydn said as a smile spread across her face. She squeezed Rosie's hand.

"When can we see her?" Rosie asked.

"Her family can go up now, but we need to speak with you. You can visit her later. An officer will escort you upstairs when you're finished answering questions."

Rosie nodded and swallowed to hold back a sob as Chief Maxwell walked away with Piper's family. The elevator door closed, leaving Rosie alone with the officers from Bear Lake County.

When Rosie slipped into the room, Piper reached out and squealed. "Rosie."

Rosie leaned in for a gentle hug. "I don't want to hurt you." She wiped a tear from her eye.

"Nothing hurts but my leg and my hip. Come here." She squeezed Rosie's hand and Rosie squeezed back.

"What happened?" Rosie sat in the chair next to Piper's bed. The Haydn family sat around the room, allowing the friends time to catch up.

"They dragged me away in their sketchy blue van. Remember, I *told* you the van was a clue."

Rosie nodded. "I'll trust your intuition next time."

Jack Haydn cleared his throat. "There will not be a next time, ladies. Am I understood?"

Piper squeezed Rosie's hand.

"Um. Yes, sir," Rosie said. She smoothed Piper's blanket. "Were you scared?"

"Yes, but they didn't treat me too badly."

Sarah scowled, and she stepped to the bed, fluffing the pillows behind Piper's head. "They didn't treat you too badly. My goodness, they kidnapped you."

"Thankfully, they didn't have much time to harm me." She smiled at Rosie. "And you know they didn't do this to me?" She pointed to her leg.

Rosie nodded. "I know! When you fell right in front of the car, I freaked out. You almost made it."

"I'm glad you got out of there. If they had kidnapped both of us, we'd still be hostages."

"I'm glad you're safe. When can you go home?" Rosie patted Piper's hand.

"Tomorrow. They're observing me tonight and waiting for the swelling in my leg to go down."

Rosie clapped her hands.

"Nice dress, by the way," Piper said, reaching out and straightening the vintage stick pin on her friend's lapel. "Cranberry Closet, I presume."

"Indeed."

Chase stood and held out a box to Rosie. "Chocolate?"

Rosie wrinkled her nose. "Eww."

"I've never understood why you dislike chocolate, Roosevelt," Sarah said, popping a square piece of candy in her mouth.

"I eat plenty of sugar, Mrs. Haydn. But I'll leave the chocolate for the rest of you. I'm nice like that."

Sarah laughed and straightened Piper's blanket.

Piper groaned, and her mother jerked her arm back. "Did I hurt you, sweetheart?"

"No. I'm sad about the *Messiah* concert. I can't lead like this," she said, waving her hand over her cast.

"Decide later," Jack said.

Braden smirked. "I nominate Rosie to lead the choir."

"Oh no," Rosie said. "You all know God didn't equip me with the voice of a nightingale." She tossed her curly hair behind her back and clasped her hands in front of her stomach. "But I can give you a little taste if you like?"

Piper giggled. "Maybe not today. My nerves are on edge."

Rosie swatted Piper's arm, but sat down. "At least we're all in agreement."

"May I come in?" Chief Maxwell popped his head into the room and tapped on the door.

Piper nodded.

Braden stood, pointing to his chair, but the chief frowned. "Sit. I'm fine." He nodded to Jack. "I have updates if you're interested."

"Please," Jack said.

Piper raised the end of the hospital bed and concentrated on the chief.

He opened a notebook and cleared his throat. "The suspects are Everett Standerwick and Lynn Miles. Mrs. Standerwick was Lynn's sister. Everett is Fergus' oldest son."

Piper nodded. "They talked about their relationship to Fergus."

"They wanted the papers you found, Rosie. Lynn demanded their return and claimed they belong to her, not Fergus. However, they're facing serious criminal charges, and are in no position to demand anything from anyone." He peered over his glasses at Piper and smiled.

Piper's stomach flip-flopped, and her eyes widened. *What in the world? Stop it.*

"Do you know what's contained in the papers? A deed? A patent?" Jack asked.

"Not yet, but one of my officers searched through the pile. Several sheets appear to be musical scores."

"Rats," Rosie said. "After all I went through, I didn't even get a peek."

"Miss Hale, I cannot condone what you did. You must not insert yourself into our investigations again."

"Amen," Jack said. "Are you two listening?" He narrowed his eyes.

"Yes, sir," Piper and Rosie said in unison.

"I have an expert coming from UW Madison tomorrow. A music professor who will give us an idea of why the suspects kidnapped you."

Piper's eyes sparkled. "Old music? Exciting. When can I take a peek?"

"Miss Haydn."

She held up her hand. "I know. I know. But if the papers end up being something special, perhaps you can allow me a glimpse?"

"No promises, but I do have news about Fergus."

Every eye in the room focused on the chief.

He smiled. "He's going to survive."

A cheer raised the roof of Piper's room, and a nurse scurried in. "Folks, please. Do I need to ask you to leave?"

"My apologies," Jack said. "We received a wonderful bit of news."

"Well, keep the noise down," she said, disappearing into the hall.

"What happened to him?" Sarah asked.

"We are waiting on toxicology reports, but the teacup might have been the clue we needed. We suspect poisoning."

Piper's eyes widened. "The woman gave me funny looking tea at the cabin," she whispered.

"Oh, my," Sarah gasped, resting her hand on her chest.

Rosie stood with her hands on her hips. "Hmm. Appears this little detective agency," she said, pointing to Piper and herself, "isn't totally off base."

"This 'detective agency' is out of business, Miss Hale." He snapped his notebook closed. "Effective immediately."

Rosie pouted and sat back down in her chair, but winked at Piper.

"Did you see that? Those two winked at each other," Chase said, pointing at the girls.

Piper stuck out her tongue. "Don't be a tattle-tale, Chase."

Chief Maxwell stood. "Sibling rivalry is above my pay grade. Fergus gave permission for me to share his condition. He'd like to extend his gratitude to you for finding him and calling for help. Although he could file a complaint, he insists he won't press charges for the breaking and entering. He's thankful his family didn't get their clutches on the papers."

Piper's jaw dropped open. "Fergus? I can't believe it."

Rosie patted Piper's hand. "Perhaps we've worked our magic on the old curmudgeon."

"Or something," Piper said. "Does Fergus know what's in the papers?"

"Apparently not. He said they belonged to his wife, and he hasn't entered her room since her passing."

"What about the Tattler blog?" Braden asked.

Chief Maxwell nodded. "Bear Lake County Sheriff's Department filed for a search warrant of their vehicle and phones. An officer is at the courthouse now, but from the comments the suspects made, we believe they wrote it."

"Explains how they knew all the details," Rosie said.

"I'm returning to Cranberry Harbor. Can I do anything for you?"

Jack Haydn stood and shook the chief's hand. "No, thank you. We appreciate your help. We've all had a long day. I believe most of us are heading back home tonight as well."

Chief Maxwell disappeared out the door, and Piper watched long after he left.

"Earth to Piper," Chase said, waving his hand in front of her eyes. "I think you've got a crush on someone."

Heat flooded Piper's cheeks, and her face flushed red. "Shut up, Chase," she said, bopping him on the arm.

"Leave her alone," Sarah said. She hid her mouth behind her hand, but spoke in her normal voice. "He *is* a fine-looking man, my dear."

"Mother!"

Sarah laughed and smiled at her family. "Who's going and who's staying here on night watch?"

Jack rose. "I have a meeting in the morning. Do you two need to head back?" he asked his sons.

"I can stay," Chase said. "Someone needs to pester Piper."

"Oh no, you don't. You go home with Dad."

Chase pouted, but Sarah motioned to the door. "It appears Rosie and I are staying?"

"If it's not too much trouble, Mrs. Haydn, since I've seen Piper with my own two eyes and know she's safe, I should get home and paint. I'm behind on the label orders and if they don't get to the printer tomorrow, I'll disappoint my customers."

"I will hold down the fort, my dear." She moved her chair close to Piper's bed and blew a kiss to her family and another one to Rosie.

"Thank you for coming," Piper said, as her father and brothers leaned over and kissed the top of her head.

Rosie kissed Piper's cheek. She put her lips on Piper's ear and whispered, "I had my fingers crossed when I promised."

Piper's eyes sparkled, and she smiled. "You're incorrigible, Roosevelt Hale."

"Yep. Exactly why you love me." She tossed her curls over her shoulder and sashayed from the room, leaving Piper giggling in her hospital bed.

When the door closed, Sarah leaned on Piper's bed. "She's an amazing friend to you, Piper. I love Rosie. But you two simply must stop this Nancy Drew business."

"She is a wonderful friend, Mom. I'm glad you love her."

"The Nancy Drew business?"

"Whatever do you mean, dear Mother?"

Sarah swatted Piper's arm. "You know what I mean." She straightened the blanket over Piper and smoothed the wrinkles. "Chief Maxwell is a good man, Piper."

Piper closed her eyes. "Mom."

"Do you think you could learn to trust him? He's nothing like Daniel."

"I'm tired, Mom. I think I should rest." Piper turned her face away from Sarah and yawned an exaggerated yawn. She smiled, thankful for safety, her family, and the best friend in the world. Would she learn to trust men? Hard to say. Would she give up the amateur detective business? Of course she would. Cranberry Harbor's crime rate offered little chance for detective work, and the odds of another strange crime seemed miniscule. She'd had more than her fair share of coincidences, but she planned to avoid investigating another murder for the rest of her life.

"Mom," she said, as Sarah dimmed the lights, "I'm glad the only murder was the destruction of the nativity figures."

"Me too, sweetheart," Sarah said, tucking the blanket around Piper's shoulders as she drifted to sleep.

CHAPTER 10

While guardian angels without number, watch you as you sweetly slumber.

.

Dream, dream, dream, of the joyous day to come.

Coda: One Week Later

Cranberry Harbor buzzed with excitement despite the winter weather. The polar vortex had moved on, and while the cold air still nipped noses and reddened cheeks, the Christkindlmarket teemed with tourists and townspeople. The Cranberry Harbor Christkindlmarket imitated the Christmas markets in Germany and Europe. Booths selling food, gifts, and handmade Christmas items filled the park.

Piper held a clipboard, checking details and radioing for help to keep market traffic moving. The pain in her hip had eased, but the cast on her leg kept her stationary. The parks and rec department built a platform in the center of the market with a comfortable chair and an ottoman for her leg. Pine garland, red ribbons, and a line of artificial Christmas trees blended her spot with the rest of the market.

Volunteers buzzed through the crowd, making sure traffic flowed smoothly and reporting to Piper interesting tidbits. A volunteer scurried past and shouted, "Dominique's gingerbread booth is open for business and a long row of children have lined up to decorate cookies."

Her stomach growled. "Someone better bring me a piece of her gingerbread," she grumbled.

Rosie skipped up the steps and plunked into the chair next to Piper. A feather from the trim on her Kelly-green wool coat floated through the air and she reached out to catch it. "These feathers keep popping off my trim." She stuffed the feather into her pocket. "I have a pile of them in here. Think I can sew them back on?"

Piper laughed. "You are very Christmas chic, my friend."

"Look," she said, pointing to a saucer-sized red poinsettia pin on her coat. "Isn't it cool?"

"It's big."

Rosie frowned. "You don't like it?"

"I love it on your coat. Tell me what you saw out there in the park."

Rosie handed Piper a tall paper cup. "Ruby sent a peppermint mocha."

Piper sipped the hot drink. "Mmm. Thanks. Tell me everything."

"The layout seems to work really well. Traffic flow is good." She held up her hand and pointed to each finger. "Face painting in progress. Chestnuts roasting. Gingerbread decorating *and* eating. Strolling choir serenading. Pretzels and bratwurst galore."

"A perfect Cranberry Harbor version of the "Twelve Days of Christmas.""

Rosie giggled. "Perhaps an original number for the community choir next year?"

"I'm sad we had to cancel the *Messiah* performance." Piper shifted in her chair.

"I think Easter is a perfect alternative. It's not your fault, you know."

"I know, but they practiced for months."

"Oh, by the way, the Haydn Music Academy performances drew an enormous crowd. Your students were a hit."

"And I missed it," Piper wailed.

"Don't give it another thought. Your teachers filled in beautifully, and who knows, maybe you'll make it over to listen before the day ends."

"Me and my scooter?"

"Or Chase can carry you on his back." Rosie giggled.

"Never in a million years. Anything else I need to know?"

"My labels look amazing on Becky and Cassidy's products. I stressed about missing the printer's deadline, but I didn't and they're fabulous. We're going to need a vacation after all this excitement."

"I'd settle for back to normal." The radio crackled, and Piper pressed the button. "Yes?"

"Don here. I'm running to the academy to get more tables for the eating area. Everyone came for pretzels at the same time. I'm taking Keegan and Logan with me, but Beckett will cover the entry booth."

"Thanks." She patted Rosie's arm. "Well, Roosevelt, I think we did it. I'm thankful for all your help."

"No problem. I'd have cried myself to sleep every night if Cranberry Harbor canceled the Christkindlmarket. It's my favorite event of the year."

Piper laughed. "Wait a minute. I thought you said the Caroling Extravaganza was your favorite. And if I search my memory, you've also claimed the Fourth of July parade, the fall Pumpkin Party, and Daffodil Derby are also your favorite events of the year."

Rosie's eyes sparkled, and she held up her palms, grinning. "What can I say? I love a good party."

Laughter rang out, and Piper looked across the park. "Skating rink seems busy, too."

"Genius of you to combine opening the rink with the Christkindlmarket. This park is hopping. Want anything?"

"I'd love a pretzel and brat if you don't mind."

Rosie hopped to her feet. "Of course not. One pretzel and bratwurst coming right up."

Piper closed her eyes, enjoying the buzz of the Christkindlmarket. Christmas carols played over the sound system, laughter filled the air, and a roving choir dressed in Dickens-era costumes added harmony to the joyful noise. Popcorn popped in a booth nearby. The scents swirled around her, reminding her of every Christmas past. The Christkindlmarket had taken so much work, but today, with a park full of neighbors celebrating their town and Christmas together, she smiled. This little slice of America she called home was worth every hour she'd spent planning.

"Excuse me, Miss Haydn. Don't want to interrupt your little nap."

Piper's eyes popped open. Chief Maxwell stood at the stairs, grinning. Her cheeks flushed. "I was not sleeping. I was enjoying the harmony of Cranberry Harbor celebrating Christmas."

He chuckled. "The clues say otherwise." He cleared his throat. "Are your parents and Miss Hale here? I have updates."

"Of course, they've all stopped by once or twice today."

"Can you call them for me? Ask if we can gather for a quick meeting, please." He peered at the clock in the center of the park. "Let's say in one hour?"

"I'll call everyone. Anything exciting?"

"I'll fill you in when we're all together. See you soon." He walked down the center aisle, an imposing figure in his uniform.

What's wrong with me? I blush when he talks to me, and I have butterflies in my stomach. He's handsome and kind. I don't trust men after Daniel, but it's time to move on or I'm going to become a spinster.

She reached for her phone to arrange the meeting between Chief Maxwell and the others. A group of children giggled as they ran past, and Piper's heart squeezed. The happiness in the air warmed her heart despite the frosty Wisconsin weather.

"Hey, boss lady," Dominique said. "I saved a special gingerbread cookie for you." She handed Piper a cookie wrapped in white paper.

Piper opened the package and held the spicy, heart-shaped cookie in the air. "Dominique, this is art. You're amazing. The white icing against the brown cookie is perfect."

"Only the best for you, sweetheart. Are you feeling alright?" Her brown eyes dimmed, and she frowned.

"I am, Dominique. Waiting for my leg to heel, but otherwise I'm good. Can't say I enjoyed the kidnapping, but I am thankful to be here on the other side of everything."

"I'm praying for you."

"Thank you."

"Better get back to my booth. Chase keeps begging me for an airplane cookie. What's gotten into your brother?"

"Dominique, if you figure him out, let us know. My parents might pay good money for information explaining Chase."

Dominique laughed, waving as she slipped away to her cookie booth, stopping to hug Rosie on the way.

Rosie scampered up the stairs and handed Piper a box. "Pretzel and brat, m'lady."

"Oh, this looks delicious. Want some?" She held the food out toward her friend.

Rosie patted her stomach. "Already had two. No room." She unbuttoned her coat and collapsed into the chair next to Piper. "What's the chief want? Another date?" She waggled her eyebrows and grinned.

"Rosie," Piper said. "Stop it."

Rosie giggled. "What did he say?"

"He has an update and wants to tell everyone at the same time."

"Perfect." She leaned back and closed her eyes. "I'm taking a snooze. I was up at stupid o'clock hustling around this park to rescue my incapacitated friend."

"And you loved every minute," Piper said.

"Indeed I did, but my eyes are tired."

Jack and Sarah Haydn climbed the steps to join the girls. Jack checked his watch. "Your brothers are on the way. What's up?"

"No idea. Chief Maxwell has an update," Piper said.

"How are you feeling, sweetheart?" Sarah asked. She reached out and felt Piper's forehead.

"Mom. I'm not sick."

"I'm your mother, dear. I can feel your forehead anytime I wish." She reached into her bag. "Look at the treat I bought at Cassidy's booth." She held up a skein of red and green speckled yarn.

"Nice. What are you knitting?"

Sarah gasped. "You know the rules. I don't need a project lined up before I buy yarn. Is there always a specific reason behind your sheet music purchases?"

"Touché, mother." Piper laughed. "Ah, the brothers." She held out her hand to Braden, and he kissed her check. "Where is your family?"

"Emily and the boys are sampling Christmas treats. I figured we could pay attention better without my noisy boys running around." His eyes gleamed, and he grinned.

"What am I, chopped liver?" Chase said, a scowl on his face.

"I'll give you a kiss. Come here." She pursed her lips and kissed the air.

He stuck out his tongue and gagged.

"Chase. We're in public," Sarah scolded.

"Before the chief arrives, I wanted to thank everyone for all your help. Especially since I'm not running at top speed these days."

"You're welcome, honey," Jack said. "Anything to benefit Cranberry Harbor is worth spending time on and, of course, so is supporting our daughter." He leaned over and kissed the top of her head. "Your team did a remarkable job."

"I think it's the best market we've ever held," Sarah said, pride beaming in her eyes.

"Ah, the people I want to see," Chief Maxwell said, sitting across from Piper.

"Chief," Jack said, reaching to shake Will's hand.

"I know you're busy. I'll make this quick." His radio crackled, and he pressed the button. "Gunther, can you handle this? I'm meeting with the Haydns. Thanks." He turned back to the group. "My apologies for the interruption."

Rosie leaned forward. "What's the news, Chief?"

He opened a file and spread it across his legs. "What do you want first? Good news or bad news?"

Piper's eyes widened. "Bad news?"

"Nothing to fear," Chief Maxwell said.

"Get the bad out of the way, please," Jack said.

The chief cleared his throat. "The toxicology report came back from the tests they ran on Fergus. He's doing well, by the way. His youngest son, Brock, took him home yesterday. You might touch base with him, Rosie. Fergus needs care until he's back on his feet."

Rosie nodded.

"What did the toxicology report say?" The empty teacup on Fergus' table flashed through Piper's mind, and a shiver ran up her spine.

He lifted the paper and read. "The lab report shows traces of the substance oleandrin and related..." He straightened his glasses and cleared his throat. "Toxic cardiac glycosides. There's other medical terms here, but you get the idea."

Piper frowned. "Toxic cardiac what?"

"What is oleandrin? Oleo?" Rosie scrunched up her face. "You mean fake butter?"

Jack tapped his chin and cleared his throat. "No, Rosie, not margarine." He turned to the chief. "Do you mean oleander poisoning?"

"Yes," Chief Maxwell said.

Sarah gasped. "What is oleander?"

The chief read from the paper. "Says here, a type of flowering shrub. All parts of the plant are highly toxic."

"Does this shrub grow in Cranberry Harbor?" Sarah asked.

"No. We are in zone four—too cold," Jack said.

Braden frowned. "How did they use a shrub to poison Fergus?"

"We suspect they served him a tea concocted from twigs and leaves of the plant," Chief Maxwell said.

Rosie's jaw dropped. "Well, well, well."

He pointed at her. "Don't get any ideas, Miss Hale."

Rosie smirked and shifted in her seat, tossing her curly hair behind her shoulder. "I'm just saying *we're* the ones who noticed it."

The chief rolled his eyes. "The tea didn't do its job, mostly because you found him and got him help in time."

"Thank God," Sarah said. "Poor Fergus."

Piper gasped and grabbed Sarah's hand. I'm so thankful I didn't drink the tea she offered me. You suspect his sister-in-law and son poisoned him?"

"They already confessed to the Bear Lake County officers."

Rosie cheered.

"I wouldn't wish that on anyone. Not even our favorite curmudgeon," Piper said.

"Why would his Fergus' son poison him?" Chase asked.

Chief Maxwell smiled. "Do you want the good news?"

Jack frowned. "An attempted poisoning is your good news?"

"Not the attempt, but the reason for the attempt is the good news." He smiled at Piper. "Are you ready?"

Rosie reached over and held Piper's hand. "We're ready," she said.

He pulled a sheet of paper from the file. "Our expert from UW Madison examined the papers you removed from Fergus' home." He smiled at Rosie. "The papers match the age of the fragments on the broken nativity scene. She called in other professionals to examine the fragments. Their report came back this morning." He paused and smiled at each person in the circle.

Piper tapped the chair arm. "Well?"

"Good thing you're sitting down, Miss Haydn. Rosie found a lost Handel manuscript worth several hundred thousand dollars."

"What?" Rosie shrieked, her eyes glowing.

Piper stared at the officer. Her mind raced and her heart pounded. "What piece?"

"At this time, they haven't identified the music, but the handwriting and age of the paper match Handel's."

"Handel? George Frideric?" Piper gasped. "Are you sure?"

"Absolutely."

"I didn't even get to lay my eyes on it," Piper wailed, and her family laughed.

"I don't understand how the nativity set ties in to this fiasco." Braden said.

"We have many questions for Mr. Standerwick, but he needs time to recuperate. His son, Brock, spoke with him briefly and from what they pieced together, the nativity set belonged to Mrs. Standerwick's family. Her ancestors brought the pieces to America when they immigrated. The paper under the finish of the shepherd contained a letter explaining everything. Mrs. Standerwick's sister knew the figures held something valuable, but didn't worry until Fergus donated the set to Cranberry Harbor. We don't know why Everett joined her quest for the family treasure, but Bear Lake

County is working on those questions. Archivists are examining the shepherd now, but the paper may not survive the removal of paint and varnish."

"What a clever way to hide information," Rosie said. "I *knew* they went together."

"Good thing you 'accidentally' dusted inside his drawers, huh?" Piper said, nudging Rosie.

"Hey, if I hadn't, those creeps would have taken off with Fergus' antique music."

"The complete story may remain a mystery we'll never solve," Chief Maxwell said.

"Ooo. A mystery?" Rosie grinned.

Chief Maxwell shook his finger. "No more mysteries for you. You either," he said, turning to Piper.

She winked at Rosie and said, "Yes, sir."

The chief closed the file and stood. "I need to get back to work, but I saved the best for last. Fergus wants to thank you two and the emergency personnel. He commissioned a replica of the nativity set, made in material a little sturdier than wood."

Piper smiled. She'd grown fond of the old set and knew the citizens of Cranberry Harbor loved it, too. "How generous. Who knew good old Fergus had a soft spot?"

"Not me," Chase said. "Now if you'll excuse me, I need to see if Dominique baked my airplane cookie."

"Leave Dominique alone," Piper said. "Why are you hounding her for an airplane cookie?"

Chase grinned. "I signed up for flying lessons, and I'm building a plane. I'll fly you to the airplane convention in Oshkosh next year."

Piper shuddered. "My goodness, Chase. The thought of climbing into a tiny aircraft with you as the pilot is my new worst nightmare."

He laughed and disappeared into the crowded Christkindlmarket.

Jack and Sarah rose. "We need to go too, sweetie. We'll see you for lunch tomorrow. You too, Roosevelt." She reached for her Chanel bag and followed Jack into the market.

"I gotta run too. Cassidy and Becky texted. Your Christmas orders are ready for pickup. I'll collect your gifts and swing by your house tonight? Should I bring my hammer to fix your squeaky step?"

Piper groaned. "I think we'll leave my security system alone, but yes, come over later. We will debrief over cookies."

Rosie saluted and walked away, her curls bobbing as she skipped through the park. Piper smiled as she watched her stop to chat with neighbors. The update from the chief had left her speechless. She couldn't believe the whole crazy mystery surrounded a missing manuscript from the very same composer she'd practiced every day for the last several months.

White lights strung around the market blinked on as the sun dimmed. Choir music sung in perfect harmony floated through the loudspeakers, and she hummed the phrase from her favorite carol. "The night is peaceful all around you. Close your eyes let sleep surround you." The beautiful music flooded her heart with joy. "God, thank you for keeping Fergus alive," she whispered.

With the mystery solved, she'd enjoy the rest of her Christmas season free of chaos. The long Wisconsin winter stretched ahead. She'd plan the spring recital soon, and the academy's busy schedule would claim her time. But she counted her blessings. Thankfully, the murder had only been the destroyed nativity scene, and not Fergus.

When spring arrived, she'd start another rehab project in her lovely Victorian home and plant flowers in her garden. Maybe Rosie would convince her to climb in yellow Bess and go glamping again. She laughed. "Nah, no more glamping. And Chase, my dear brother, I'll never go flying with you. Never."

To catch up Piper and Rosie's other adventures, check out The Piper Haydn Piano Mystery Series—*Murder Goes Solo* & *Murder Goes Glamping* at my book shop—search for **shopmalissachapin**

A Piper Haydn Piano Mystery
Murder Goes
Glamping
MALISSA
CHAPIN

MURDER GOES CAROLING
PLAYLIST

***Handel's Messiah**

***Still, Still Still**

***Joy to the World**

ACKNOWLEDGEMENTS

Thank you to:

***Brian McCrorie**— for helping me get the melisma details correct.

***Christine Krueger**—for helping me with German and science terms.

***Deb Rohrkaste**—for sharing a fun tourist attraction in Dubai

***Luke Hawley**—for helping me hammer out story details. You're a great brainstorming buddy.

***M. Brian Smith, Communications Supervisor, Winnebago County, Wisconsin Sheriff's Department, Oshkosh, Wisconsin**—for making sure I got dispatcher details correct.

***My Alpha Team**—Crystal Thornton, Mary McGlone, Laurie Herlich, Christina Lyon, Shelly Smith, Tricia Troyer, Rebekah Kotlar, Marsha Landro, Karla Bolender, Jackie Koll, Rachel Hershberger, John Bonner, Carrie Petersen, Erica Waggoner, and Kristie Van Zanten. Thank you for making me work hard to write a better story.

***My favorite Keegan, Logan, and Beckett**—for being excited about Aunt Malissa's books. I love you.

**My family*—for helping me with ideas, vetoing the bad ones, and listening to my rambles. I love you.

**You*—for joining Piper and Rosie on another adventure.

Sweetberry's Gingergread Cookies

(Yield 24 cookies made with a 5" cutter)

2 c. all purpose flour
1/2 tsp. salt
1/2 tsp. baking soda
1 tsp. baking powder
1 tsp. ginger
1 tsp. cloves
1 1/2 tsp. cinnamon
1/2 tsp. nutmeg
1 c. shortening
1/2 c. sugar
1/2 c. molasses
1 egg yolk

Instructions:

1. Mix the dough early in the morning to allow it time to chill.

2. Sift the flour with salt, baking powder, baking soda and spices.

3. In a large bowl, cream shortening with sugar and molasses until light and fluffy. Beat in egg yolk and flour mixture.

4. Refrigerate dough all day.

5. Roll dough out onto a lightly floured surface. Cut out gingerbread cookies and place on an ungreased baking sheet.

6. Bake at 350 degrees Fahrenheit for 8-10 minutes or until done.

7. Allow to cool before removing from the baking sheet.

8. Decorate and enjoy.

Thank you for coming along on another adventure with Piper and Rosie. I hope you enjoy these ladies, their town and their neighbors as much as I do.

I'm honored that you took the time to read my story!

If you'd like to read more about George Frideric Handel, check out the book written by his friend. *Memoirs of the Life of the Late George Frideric Handel* by John Mainwaring.

If you have missed the first two Piper Haydn Piano Mysteries, you can find *Murder Goes Solo & Murder Goes Glamping* at my book shop— Search for Shopmalissachapin

About the Author

Malissa Chapin has a heart for writing stories filled with humor, faith, and truth. She's always adored reading excellent books and is tickled to see her childhood dream of becoming an author finally come true.

Malissa loves creating with words, watercolor, fabric, and yarn. You can find her in her garden, at the piano, homeschooling her bonus baby, or enjoying a coffee with friends. She lives and sometimes freezes in Wisconsin with her family and a crazy cat.

9 781965 414002